Other Work
by Beverly G

CW00383000

NOVEL
Concrete Wings
Historical Fiction

A naïve teen sent out of Cuba to retrieve smuggled family jewels on the eve of the Bay of Pigs Invasion comes of age in New York City at the height of the sexual revolution and earns his political and economic freedom. By a twist of fate, he begins to lose his liberty when his oppressive parents arrive and refuse to assimilate into American Society. (Reader's Five Star Favorite and Literary Classics Seal of Approval with recommendation for home and school libraries)

SCREENPLAYS
Concrete Wings
Family Drama/Coming of Age

A naïve teen sent out of Cuba to retrieve smuggled family jewels on the eve of the Bay of Pigs Invasion comes of age in New York City at the height of the sexual revolution and earns his political and economic freedom. By a twist of fate, he begins to lose his liberty when his oppressive parents arrive and refuse to assimilate into American Society.

Misinformed Heart
Drama:

A prescription addicted environmentalist on the verge of success and marriage is wrongly accused of murder as she struggles to overcome an incestuous past.

SCREENPLAYS
continued

Rent Money
Comedy:

While working in the Radio and TV barter business for two sexually active bosses, a self-sufficient, virgin bookkeeper, aroused by a handsome neighbor, is stymied by society's changing rules as the sexual revolution engulfs Manhattan in 1965. (Winner of the Golden Palm Award for Best Screenplay at the 2012 Beverly Hills International Film Festival.)

Turnaround
Co-written with John Han

Family Drama:

A financier's Asian discipline and love of music frees his Spanish stepson from the gut wrenching effects of ADD to become an A student and world class musician.

Unprotected Witness
Co-written with Jack Knight

Drama/Thriller:

In 1994, a young wife who relocates to AZ from NY for health reasons, is subjected to relentless sexual advances by a dangerous retiree with a hidden criminal past. In a battle for survival, by her own resourcefulness and the wonders of the Internet, she derails an impending attack, positions the bully to meet his destiny and triumphs in secret.

While I Wait
Drama:
Inspired by a true story. As the AIDS Virus spread in the 1980's,
New Yorkers were gripped with fear anxiety and ignorance. Being
an administrative assistant to a prominent attorney with AIDS was
easy; being his friend, well that was hard.

Coming Soon:
NON-FICTION BOOK

Women, Work and Triumph
Interviews with fascinating women.

Author's Website:
www.bevgandara.com

SOARING IN SILENCE

One Woman's Triumph Over Fear

By Beverly Gandara

Soaring in Silence

Copyright © 2019
Beverly Gandara

Author website
www.bevgandara.com

Back cover photo of Beverly Gandara
by George Atoraya Simonov.

ISBN:
Paper Back: 978-0-9971406-2-0
Hard Cover: 978-0-9971406-3-7

Prose Press
Pawleys Island, SC
prosencons@live.com

Dedication:

For Armand, simply the love of my life.
Thank you for your support and unconditional love.

To the loving memory of my parents, Irene and Stanley,
gone too soon.

Acknowledgments:

The people named below have all generously contributed their time and talent to the betterment of this novel.

With gratitude to Jack Knight, veteran actor of stage, screen and television, and a delightful writing partner with whom I co-wrote Unprotected Witness, a screenplay, which inspired this novel.

With appreciation for Bob O'Brien, publisher for his guidance and expertise in compiling and organizing the work into a readable format.

With love and affection for my editor, Honora Levin for her brilliance, patience and friendship.

With admiration for James Petrucci, artist who permitted me to use his lovely art creation for the cover.

With many thanks to Bruce Feigenbaum for his continued support and vision for the cover design.

With respect to Lieutenant George Prunes, Union City, N.J., Police Dept., Retired for his sharp eyes and skill as a proof reader.

With great fondness for my early readers; Alexandra Rich, Marketing Professional, AJG and Ms. M who choose to remain anonymous.

1
Kim and Brad Wolf-1994

Kim and Brad Wolf are a handsome couple, late forties; she, a pretty woman with big brown eyes and long blond curly hair short in stature with a slim curvy figure; he is average height and weight, handsome face with dark brown hair and hazel eyes. They are conservative in their dress and behavior. Manners are important to them. They work hard, are devoted to their families, and simply adore each other.

During the Summer after a one-week vacation which changes their lives forever, Kim and Brad return home to their co-op apartment in Manhattan and make the decision to move across country. Having lived in New York all of her life, Kim hasn't visited that many places which impress her as much as Arizona. Then again, she isn't much of a traveler.

They're charmed by the beauty of the mountains against the spectacular ever-changing skies; the quiet of the colorful desert and the respect for the land of all its people. One can think there and grow from the inside out, while in contrast to Manhattan with all its excitement, energy, noise and constant movement, it seems all knowledge comes from the outside in.

Kim and Brad leave family and friends wondering why they are relocating to a place where they know no one, have no support systems and have visited for one week only. It's easy. To paraphrase Dr. Samuel Johnson, England's prolific writer and philosopher, "When a man is about to be hanged, it concentrates the mind wonderfully." You see, after nine years of medical tests and unexplained illness at the age of forty-nine, Kim has been diagnosed with Takayasu's Arteritis, a rare form of Vasculitis and given one year to live.

Brad is in a state of disbelief, perhaps denial. Kim is angry and defiant; how could this happen now? She is so happy and in love. Their lives are thrilling – the world is endlessly fascinating. She demands of herself more time and has no intention of fulfilling that medical prophecy. Life expectancy in 1994 is 75.7 years. She adds twenty years and makes that her goal.

Kim knows she needs to rest her mind, body and soul. With her faithful husband Brad by her side, she knows instinctively that she can accomplish anything to which she sets her mind. She vows to fight, and Arizona offers her the peaceful environment in which to meet the battle head on.

2

Kim and Brad's Adventure Begins

After tearful good-byes to family and friends they arrive in beautiful Arizona. Their rental apartment is crisp and clean. They are its first occupants. It is spacious and easy to maintain. There is an exercise facility on the premises and since Kim is encouraged by her New York physicians to walk at least thirty minutes a day she does her best on a treadmill and rests before and after as necessary while Brad is at work. Her balance is off; her walking is becoming more and more difficult. She presses on.

Kim had been employed as an Administrative Assistant to high level executives. The jobs paid, well, required organizational, financial, managerial and diplomatic skills and prolonged hours. It was a privilege for her to work for some of Manhattan's most prestigious leaders of profit and non-profit organizations. It is difficult to say good-bye to her work life and a Herculean adjustment to give up the daily challenges and triumphs as well as her paycheck.

Kim is excited by technology as it continues to evolve with the release of Apple's PowerPC Microprocessor Macintosh personal computer. During the day her personal computer is her focus. Unable to commit to full-time work she has the world at her fingertips. Early in her career, she was taught not to consider something as factual until she found it in at least three different publications. Kim reads a lot.

Brad is in sales. He requested and was granted a transfer to the Arizona office of his company and continues his benefits and pension.

He works part time at buying and selling antiques, collectibles and vintage wrist watches. Brad's dream is to convert his many hobbies into a full-time business and for Kim the goal is paramount. Why not do it all? Move, take control of their health, start a new business and buy a house. She is fearless. Brad is worried but denies her nothing and graciously supports her in their accelerated plans.

The Internet is new, and she is eager to start Brad's business online. Brad is happier to rent space in a newly established antique center to sell his antiques, collectibles and vintage wrist watches. Kim continues to research Internet possibilities and is enthused about the prospect of doing both.

Kim longs to search for a new home. Brad asks her to rest before they start the enormous task of searching, finding and moving into a new home. He is adjusting to his job transfer, while trying to start his new business and they are adapting to the move. As always, the voice of reason she agrees. She is convinced they have plenty of time to move again.

The money from the sale of their co-op apartment is in the bank earning interest and they are comfortable in their new surroundings. Perhaps Brad is just waiting to see how her health progresses and does not want to make a commitment he cannot handle.

Anchored to her computer she realizes she needs to get out of the house more often and find other activities to keep her busy. She researches volunteer opportunities and is delighted to discover the city has a designated volunteer office; she makes an appointment with City's Volunteer Coordinator to see how she could utilize her skills and perhaps do some good for her new community. Brad is fine with that.

They are happy and make sure to celebrate their new life with each passing day. They are settling in peacefully.

3
Jack Oviatt's Peace Interrupted

BOOM! It is 2:00 a.m.; the temperature is 100 degrees. Most people are asleep in the small, quiet Arizona desert town outside of Phoenix until the explosion wakes up the populace. I literally jump out of my bed and as I hastily dress, the phone rings, and the desk sergeant gives me the address.

My name is Jack Oviatt. With two weeks left until my retirement from an Arizona police force after thirty years of service, I've been sleeping later, taking it easy, trying to acclimate myself to not working. There are no open cases, my paperwork is up to date and I'm blissfully gliding through the last couple of weeks by biding my time before I take over the city police volunteer program.

I'm on scene within minutes, the adrenaline coursing through every inch of my body. This is my last chance to exercise my skills and feel needed. I'm pumped. As I stare up at the two-story building and marvel as the front half of the 1994 dark cherry metallic Cadillac DeVille teeters perilously on the ledge of the second-floor window, I know immediately what happened. Too much damned dynamite!

It makes sense. A couple of weeks ago there was a report about stolen dynamite from a construction site near an old abandoned silver mine.

The heavy stench of wreckage from the charred building hangs in the air in the oppressive heat. After the fire crews extinguish the small fires caused by the detonation and the bomb squad finishes their inspection in the smoky rubble to make sure there are no secondary explosives planted, I conclude that it was done either by an amateur or someone wanting to send a message. It gives a new definition to overkill.

The violent burst blew out windows in at least half a dozen buildings in the middle of the block in the commercial area. The few people injured by flying glass and debris are visitors staying at the local motel. They're treated at the scene; most are sent back to their rooms. Two are transported to the hospital.

Generally, the street activity is at a minimum, traffic is light, but *everyone* wants to know what happened. Curious, frightened and excited people rush to the scene via bicycles, cars, on foot, horses, motorcycles and trucks. Some folks are hastily dressed in mismatched clothes, some still in pajamas and robes, many carrying crying babies and young children. Several bring their pets. It is an exciting event, a loud chaotic happening! The noise is deafening. Barking dogs, people shouting questions, giving opinions and demanding answers barely drown out the wail of the sirens from the police, fire and rescue and ambulances, as well as snorting horses, motorcycles and revved up trucks.

Soon after my arrival, our mayor, Josiah Harris arrives on scene and immediately tries to quell the noisy outbursts. A popular mayor, Josiah is trustworthy and congenial; he is a good ole boy known as everybody's friend. He is as round as he is short-about 5'3". His rotund stature is exaggerated by the white linen suits he wears daily with a different vibrant solid colored shirt. His little beady eyes loll behind small round rimless blue lensed sunglasses. To cover an ever expanding bald spot, he always wears a white fedora hat with a feather fastened to a black band, tilted to the right side of his head like a nineteen fifties crooner. Every day he happily makes his way through town-always available to anyone with a concern, complaint or question. With his jolly aura, high-pitched voice and sing song manner he repeats "I'm just another concerned citizen doing what's best for the community."

This is during his third term as mayor. I watch him drenched in sweat as he labors with little information to reassure us that we are all safe and this is an isolated incident. Newspaper, television and radio reporters are quick to set up their equipment and interview him. "Probably a structural defect of some kind." He tries unsuccessfully to sell that line, but no one is buying it.

"Boo! We want answers!" The loutish mob refuses to disperse. Reporters move through the mass of people and interview anyone who has something to say. Mayor Harris is left to fend on his own. He desperately tries to calm the querulous group. Switching to campaign mode, he makes eye-contact with several people in the crowd, waves to many and raises his hands up and down to quiet them. With hand to heart and bowed head, he continues as if he were giving a sermon.

"My friends, there is no truth to the rumor that this was a bomb. If it was, it would be our first. We will let the investigators scrutinize the damage and give their report before we draw any conclusions."

He punches the air for emphasis as he shouts, "Proof! We need proof of what happened and that my friends, takes time, lots of time. I suggest you all go home now and let our highly trained personnel do their work."

Mayor Harris blusters through the unruliness shouting above the din with a forced smile blinding us with the sheen of his overly bleached whitened teeth, hands flying for emphasis. Many leave the area as requested. Some linger. Those who don't trust him stay, arms folded, watchful eyes analyzing every move made by the squad of investigators. Fear and anger rule the night.

It is all hands on deck. fire fighters rescue workers and police work together cooperatively. I labor long into the next day alongside local fire inspectors and police investigators, sifting through the rubble collecting samples of whatever needs to be examined more closely. We have to determine if the car was used as a weapon to destroy the building or if the vehicle and its occupant(s), if any, are victims.

Auto parts and body parts are scattered on the roofs of adjoining buildings and on the street below. It is-messy, very messy. I am right about the dynamite. Whoever did this used enough to blow a car weighing almost 4,000 pounds ten feet up and back into the narrow two-story office building.

The second story is demolished. Electrical wires hang from the ceiling, sparks are flying out the busted fluorescent lights. The water pipes are broken and spewing cascades of water everywhere. The furniture is ruined, the carpets are soiled, and water damaged, office equipment destroyed.

The wrecked commercial building is immediately deemed uninhabitable and sealed off by the building inspector.

As I am about to leave the second floor, I look out the window and watch the crowd disperse. My senses on alert always. I make judgments about people in seconds, trust no one and assume everyone is lying. That's when I see him. Shadow Man. He is dressed in black, wearing dark sunglasses in the middle of the night. I notice him among the crowd because he's talking into what looks like a brick with an antenna, sort of like a military walkie talkie and covering the mouthpiece as he speaks. He is totally out of place in behavior and dress. I motion to one of the younger officers on the street to question him. He doesn't understand me, and I lose the opportunity as Shadow Man disappears from sight.

4

Shadow Man

A tall figure dressed in black, wearing dark sun glasses moves stealthily to an alleyway near the demolished building. He's young, late twenties, slim but muscular with black straight hair and smooth olive skin. He removes his sun glasses, momentarily allowing his dark piercing eyes to scan the street before he speaks into his smart phone It is a calendar, address book, clock, a notepad, has email and a keyboard with an integrated radio modem, a very expensive and heavy gadget. Basically, it is a PDA. called the IBM Simon Personal Communicator. His boss, a high tech junkie makes sure he has the latest and best equipment on the market.

Glass and debris crackle under his feet as he ducks into a doorway, leans against the wall and whispers, "Boss, no disrespect here, but you sent me cross country to do a job. It took me a week to find him. I know where he works, and I know where he lives. So, why'd you send someone else to get rid of him?"

The Boss, a fat cigar chomping white haired man dressed in Armani, loves technology. He sits behind a large heavy dark mahogany desk with an open IBM computer which has a Pentium microprocessor.

The gravelly voice with a Brooklyn accent questions, "Someone else? Whaddya talkin' about?"

"But, Boss. It's a beaut! I'm lookin' at what's left of his Cadillac. Its hangin' half way out a window on the second story of the building where he worked. The building looks like it's going to collapse. I'm tellin' ya', if he was in his car or the building, they're gonna need a vacuum cleaner to find him." Shadow Man crosses himself, kisses his fingers and adds. "May he rest in pieces!"

"You stay put! I'm gonna make some calls and find out who did this." The Boss paces back and forth, thinking out loud. Shadow Man waits patiently for further instructions. He knows never to hang up until The Boss gives his permission. He stands in the alley tapping his foot. He is eager to move. He's pretty sure someone from the second floor of the damaged building is staring at him. He moves further into the shadows. After a few minutes, The Boss speaks.

"Listen, this is what I want you to do. Get over to his apartment right now before the cops identify the car and find him dead or alive. He always kept lists, had a bad habit of writing everything down. See what you can find, photos, newspaper clippings, notes, whatever. Call me from there."

"Got it, Boss."

Fifteen minutes later, Shadow Man breaks into an apartment and searches it as instructed. He calls The Boss.

The Boss eagerly grabs the phone. "Talk to me."

"Boss, I'm here at his apartment, but it looks like somebody got here before me. The place is a mess."

"Did you find anything we can use?"

"Just a couple of torn bank money wrappers on the floor. No books, notes, nothin', just a lot of garbage. The guy was a pig."

"I didn't ask for your opinion on his personal habits. Go back to your motel, sniff around for information and wait for my instructions."

"Yes, Boss."

Shadow Man returns to the motel near the scene of the explosion. He roams through the street listening for tidbits from police conversations and lingers in the lobby of the motel to listen to all the gossip. When he's heard enough, he returns to his room and takes a nap.

Two hours later, the Boss calls.

"Whaddya find out?"

"They haven't recovered a body, yet. The building is condemned, the whole street is blocked off, no traffic. The cops are still there, and the investigators are gonna work through the night. It's gonna take them a long time to figure out what happened. So, can I come home?"

"No. I want you to stay put."

"Why?"

"When the cops are finished with his apartment, I want you to rent it or another one in same the building."

"Why?"

"Willie had an ongoing poker game. You continue the game."

"Why?"

"What are you – ten years old? Stop asking so many questions and do what I say."

"Sorry, Boss. I know you're planning something."

"I have a feeling Willie found a big rat with a hefty contract on his head and I wanna collect."

"You mean John Banion?"

"Talk to the guys Willie played poker with and get a description of all the players. Then you're going to work for the limo company run by Gino, one of our guys. He keeps the airport watch and knows who flies in and out of Arizona. That's important."

"So, when can I come home?" Shadow Man begs.

"When I tell ya. Call me every day with a progress report."

"On it, Boss."

5

Kim's Day Out

Kim's appointment with the volunteer coordinator is in the late afternoon. She has several hours to explore downtown as a tourist.

As she rides Ollie the Trolley, she notices two men riding in the back deeply engaged in conversation. One about forty-five, dressed in a suit and tie looks like a slick spiritless professional of some sort. He carries a bulging briefcase and rests it on his lap.

His companion, she estimates to be between seventy-five to eighty, looks like a brooding bushy-haired brute with a menacing scowl. He wears a baseball cap, large sunglasses and keeps his head down so she can't see him too well. He is dressed in black slacks and a black tee shirt with lettering. All she can see is K I G A. It makes no sense to her. He's loud. She detects a Brooklyn accent. They seem out of place. She dismisses them as tourists and doesn't pay any more attention to them.

Besides the two out of place men, there are about a dozen tourists listening to the driver/guide with disposable cameras at the ready. She is about sixty-five, a happy grandmother who announces over the microphone how she loves her job and provides them with a wealth of information about the history of downtown Scottsdale and its fascinating sights. Kim tries to listen to her running commentary.

"In 1888, Army Chaplain, Winfield Scott purchased large tracts of land bordering Scottsdale Road for two dollars and fifty cents per acre…"

The animated conversation between the two men is momentarily distracting. Kim has difficulty hearing the guide. She refocuses and begins to absorb the energy of the city that is to become her new home.

The trolley loops through downtown and Old Town Scottsdale so there are many opportunities to get on and off at several stops to visit all the attractions that part of the city offers. It is time to explore the many shops and art galleries, so with several other passengers she exits the trolley. She is using a cane and welcomes the several benches available amid the activity of the streets.

Scottsdale was recently voted one of the best cities in which to live. She understands why. It is clean, exquisite and the sun shines every day. As an added bonus there are plenty of jobs in the "right to work state."

Tourism is a large part of the economy so courtesy and respect are a welcomed part of the fabric of behavior amongst the diversified population. The charm of Old Town Scottsdale featured as The West's Most Western Town reminds her of all the westerns she saw as a kid. Western-style boots belts and hats, Kachina dolls and silver and turquoise jewelry are the main attraction. There are many crafts by artisans from local Indian tribes. Wishing to know more about the tribes and the Kachina dolls, she buys a book, a bracelet and for Brad a heavy silver belt buckle. She could hear him say as he always does when he picks up a gold watch and holds it, "Feel the money!"

Kim enjoys wandering through the quaint shops. She makes note of an historic movie theater with the neon sign reminiscent of the nineteen fifties. Hungry and thrilled to discover an old-fashioned ice cream parlor, Kim indulges in an ice cream sundae prepared and presented with the attention one expects for a $100.00 meal. In fact, the service everywhere they go is impeccable. Kim and Brad are in awe as workers routinely refuse tips and request a letter of commendation instead. She plans to bring Brad to all the sights.

6
City Volunteer Office

Kim is impressed by the spacious, clean and light government offices.

The City Volunteer Coordinator, James about thirty is tall, thin balding and bespectacled. He runs a well-organized, vital operation and appears to be serious and warm. They shake hands.

"Tell me Mrs. Wolf, why do you want to volunteer?"

"I have the time, hopefully the talent you need and a desire to help."

"Please sit while I review your application."

She sits patiently.

"We have a group of strong healthy (he hesitates, while he makes note of her cane and continues) economically independent retirees in Arizona. There are many retired military – male and female. The opportunities to volunteer are limitless. City volunteers are highly respected and treated quite well," he proudly announces.

"Does my use of a cane create a problem?" she asks.

"Not at all. Please forgive my obvious clumsiness. I was thinking about having you stand on your feet for long periods of time, but it appears the positions available do not require that and clearly you are well-qualified. There are several vacancies at the hospital and the police department."

Kim takes a moment to mull over the opportunities.

The police department sounds fascinating."

"I am sure it is and because of your computer skills you will be

14

involved with data entry."

"That sounds appealing."

"Good."

James makes some notes on a piece of paper and places it in her file.

"I'll arrange a meeting with Jack Oviatt, our new police volunteer coordinator and have him contact you directly. Thank you for coming in."

They shake hands. Kim heads home happy.

7

Kim's Peace Interrupted

Kim enters the same crowded trolley on her way home. To her surprise the two mysterious out-of-place men are in the same seats engaged in deep conversation and seemingly oblivious to those around them. The only seat available to her is behind a pole close to the two men. She hears them intermittently but her view of them is partially obscured by the pole as is their view of her.

The same sweet bus driver/guide continues her spiel. She talks about the Little Red Schoolhouse built in 1910. It contains two rooms and she explains that all children of every age attended. The female teacher a single lady by requirement taught all grades. According to the guide once she married her teaching days ended. Kim wants to know more about that but is distracted by the two men.

The Suit removes a small crematory urn from the briefcase on his lap and hands it to the Brute.

"Rosa's ashes," he says respectfully.

"Forty years of marriage and this is what I get?"

The guide continues her talk over the microphone, but attention is directed to the two men as the elder man's voice is raised in anger.

"I'm sorry," seems to be all the Suit is able say.

"You were supposed to send them to her family!"

"I was overruled; you know, a chance it might get traced back!"

If Kim hears the Suit correctly, she wonders what that means. The two men now have everyone's attention and Kim is as intrigued as the guide and the other tourists. All eyes are on them.

16

The Brute opens the urn and precipitously dumps the ashes out of the window, barely missing strolling tourists. He then tosses the urn back to the Suit. The Suit catches it but drops his briefcase in the process. Papers scatter. He scrambles to pick them up.

"My God!" he utters incredulously.

"I ain't the sentimental type!" booms the Brute.

There is a collective gasp. All the passengers are horrified and stunned into silence.

The guide unexpectedly stops the trolley and remains in her seat. She lifts the microphone and in a stern voice, shouts, "Gentlemen! This is a tourist trolley. Perhaps you would like to exit the vehicle here and take your business elsewhere."

The Suit, still struggling to reorganize his papers, apologizes.

"Sorry folks. 'Just a minor misunderstanding."

"Hell, I'm not sorry!" The Brute smirks. "What are you all looking at?" He makes a scary face and roars like a lion.

The Brute slaps his knee and laughs out loud. "Did you see that? Scared the hell out of them!"

The Suit gives him a nasty look and whispers through gritted teeth, "Cut it out!"

The Brute lowers his laughter to a barely audible twitter.

Many of the tourists leave their seats. One rings the bell several times in a panic. The Guide opens the door and quite a few people rush off the trolley. Far from her destination. Kim curls into her seat behind the pole.

The Suit again apologizes. He is embarrassed. "My apologies folks. Ma'am. Please continue. There will be no more interruptions," the Suit assures the guide.

She drives to the corner and welcomes a new group of tourists. By the time Kim decides to change her seat it is too late. The seats fill up quickly.

What a strange couple of men Kim thinks to herself.

The two men settle back in their seats and continue their

conversation quietly. Kim has to strain to listen but hears only fragments of their discussion. While she focuses on the guide's fascinating facts about life in the desert in the early 1900's, the two men continue their dialogue.

Suit: "Give me the papers." The Brute hands the Suit a set of papers. The Suit reviews them.

Suit: "You and your panty raids." He is clearly disgusted.

Brute: "We were kiddin' around and she got coy on me. So, I gave her what she asked for, a lick and a promise."

"It says here you grabbed the Activities Director, Mitzi Benson and touched her inappropriately."

"So, I felt her up a little."

Kim is uncomfortable and eager to get home. They continue and she listens.

"Ever since Rosa died, you're like a hyena in heat."

"You're dead, you're dead! I miss gettin' it regular."

"This is the second sexual harassment complaint we received."

"You took care of it with that Lydia broad! Right?"

"You're lucky she cooperated and took our deal." The Brute makes an exaggerated smile.

"See my teeth, I'm grateful."

"You'd better hope this one is as accommodating."

"Just throw a little money at her and she'll open her legs too."

Tourists get on and off at various stops. The guide continues her dialogue over the microphone. "In 1920, a cotton gin opened at the corner of Second Street and ..."

The Suit lectures, "I'm warning you. It's the women who will do you in. Get your brains out of your boxers and find someone who thinks you're irresistible."

The Brute replies, "They all do. But it's this place. I'm bored! There's no action. Even the casinos are boring."

"I told you to stay away from anyplace you may run into people who knew you."

"Too late!"

"Damn it! Who recognized you?"

"Willie the Weasel, a nobody. He won't cause me any trouble."

"You do nothing without reporting to me, understand?"

"Sure, sure. You'll protect me."

"That's my job. Now you are in enough trouble with these harassment complaints, so I suggest you find a hobby."

"I don't need no hobby."

"You gotta behave or we let you go."

The Brute raises his voice and becomes quite animated.

"Get me out of this ashtray or take out your Roscoe and put one right here!" The Brute leans over and puts his fore finger between his eyes.

Kim hears that part clearly - the rest had been muddled. She prays they can't see her. She buries her face in a writer's magazine she always carries with her and crouches as low as she can in the seat.

Thankfully the Brute and the Suit exit the trolley at the next stop. What has she witnessed? The trolley continues and within a short time she arrives home thinking no longer about the two strange men.

8

Jack's Retirement

My retirement, like my childhood was short.

I was offered an opportunity to work for the city and I took it. It keeps me busy organizing and supervising volunteers for local police departments. We have a lot of retired professionals and ex-military who want to work and give back to the community. They save us hundreds of man-hours and thousands of dollars; we are happy to have them.

Supervising the volunteers takes me around to all the police departments so I am always in touch with the latest happenings without putting my life on the line. I'm busy but frankly a bit weary. I miss the action.

I loved being a LEO (Law Enforcement Officer). It motivated me, the excitement of it, the camaraderie with the guys at work. That's the action I craved. That's where I could be myself, talk about anything to any of the guys despite the fact that we sometimes fought and competed, but we never got bored. They had my back in any situation and I had theirs.

I've saved my share of lives. I got plenty of bad guys off our streets, delivered two babies and served my community well. But after thirty years of dealing with the worst society has to offer, one cannot undo what the eyes have seen, the nose has smelled, or the heart has felt after witnessing unimaginable torment. I had enough of dead babies, raped teenagers, beaten wives, stabbings, shootings, drugs and gangs. It is time to play and discover what "normal" feels like.

Being a LEO is hard on the body, mind and soul. Although I am basically in good shape, the long hours, skipped meals and physical requirements were a challenge. I'm in my late fifties, tall, agile and financially secure. My mind is sharp, my senses heightened but my body is on turtle time.

I knew it was time to retire when I after an evening of dining and dancing, I automatically put my date in the back seat and pushed down on her head as if she were a criminal I was escorting back to the station. She still won't take my call.

Before my retirement, I started each day at five o'clock a.m. with a six mile run, shower and shave. I favor khaki shorts and golf shirts. I continue my daily morning routine and goal to stay in shape, not for work but to outrun an early death as age is creeping up on me. I need to know I can heal quickly. There is no one to take care of me. I live alone.

Women are a mystery to me. I just don't understand them, their values, motives, emotions, all of it – none of it. I don't know, nor any longer care to know how to connect with them and their specific brand of intelligence. I've rarely come across a woman I could hold a decent conversation with, including my wives. Trust. It's the one thing I could never find in a woman. So, I stopped looking.

I love sex with them, but I can't live with them. I tried. I married and divorced once, have an adult child and two grandchildren and remarried a great gal. She was much younger than I, maybe too young. We really did not have too much in common. She was exactly my type physically, tall, dark and lean. Unfortunately, she was killed in a car accident by a drunk driver who also perished. We were only married a short time. I often wonder what my life would have been like if she were still here. Would we have had kids?

My soul is like a deep, dark empty cavern with echoes and whispers of voices I barely hear. That's why I stay busy, running, hiking, anything to avoid coming home to an empty nest. My daughter suggested I get a dog and gave me the name of a shelter that rescues dogs.

While law enforcement has been my life's work, outdoor sports is my passion. Arizona's lakes, forests, mountains and desert are perfect for boating, camping, hiking, cycling and golf. I indulge in all of it and have all the sports equipment to support my athletic activities stored neatly in my three-car garage. My 1994 Jeep Wrangler gets me to wherever I need to be to play. Rather than stay in a fancy hotel, I prefer to sleep outdoors surrounded by nature with the moon as my pillow and stars as my blanket.

9

Kim Meets Jack

It only took a few weeks after my retirement before my boredom turned to drudgery. Supervising volunteers just isn't all that exciting. I explored other opportunities; there aren't any positions available, so I'll stay. I've got one more interview today.

Kim waits patiently as Jack reviews her application. He seems serious and efficient. Although he is head of the volunteers, she senses he had a more important position before retirement from whatever it was, he had done.

He is older than she, healthy, tanned and fit. His neatly cut full head of hair, once dark is now a mixture of dark and grey and nicely frames high cheekbones and vivid blue eyes. She would say he had a ruggedly handsome face, well suited to a movie loner type hero. He is the kind of man who saves the town from the bad guys, but who cannot commit to the one woman who loves him.

His brusque manner is that of a military officer in charge and she finds him a bit intimidating. He makes some notes on a yellow pad and abruptly closes her file.

Kim must be about fifty. She is a little bit of a thing, maybe 5' 110 pounds, blond nice figure with eyes the color of hot cocoa on a cold Christmas eve. As long as she has no agenda other than a commitment to work. we can use her expertise.

"You seem to have a solid work background. I know we can use your computer skills; we're installing a new program throughout the department. You may have to work in several different areas," Jack notes.

"Anywhere is fine with me. I am here to help."

"Good," he states with conviction. "You will have to be finger-printed, photographed, required to take a lie detector test, vetted by the FBI and interviewed by a high-ranking officer before you will be allowed to work on our computers."

"I understand."

"If you go through the process and are accepted, I want you to know that while working at the precinct, if you dare to use any information you hear or see for your own or someone else's benefit, it would be considered a felony. You will be arrested and spend time in prison. Is that clear?"

"Absolutely!"

He lowers his tone. "You see, we had a young volunteer who had access to the computers and a boyfriend who had a couple of speeding tickets. He convinced her that with a touch of the delete button, she could erase his criminal history. Out of blind, misguided love, she deleted his record. The boyfriend, now quite confident with his contact in the police department promised his friends he could do the same for them for a fee and started a small cottage industry.

He threatened the girl that he would report her if she did not comply. She was compromised by what she thought was love and her own criminal actions. Within a short time, she was caught, arrested and convicted. She will spend an inordinate amount of time in prison while the boyfriend has moved on to a new girlfriend."

The story was finished. "Message received," Kim declares.

"Good. I will let you know if you're application has been accepted. If so, I will arrange for you to be finger-printed and photographed. If all goes well, you will be scheduled for a lie detector test and if you pass, you will be interviewed by a high-ranking officer. The process may take some time."

"I understand."

10

The Lie Detector Test

Kim is not nervous but excited and curious. She sits in a small windowless room and waits for a man named Jason. The equipment is on the table. She is fascinated by the buttons, wires and straps. Jason crashes through the door and startles her. He is big, maybe 50 pounds overweight; it is all in the stomach. He is tall, balding with black stringy hair tied in a ponytail. His mustache almost reaches his Elvis sideburns. He stares at her; no through her with hooded dark eyes.

Kim attempts to introduce herself. "Hello, I am …"

"I know who you are, let's get started." Courtesy and manners are not part of his personality.

"I'm going to hook you up, ask several questions, then we will repeat the questions. You may be here for a while, so relax."

Kim sits back and places her cane alongside the chair. Does she detect a moment of pity?

"Is it okay if I put the cane in the corner?" Jason lamely inquires.

"Yes," she responds quietly.

He straps her in and hooks her up to the machine. "Is Kim your first name?" he begins.

"Yes," she says in a strong voice.

He follows up with additional generic questions, watches the machine closely and makes notes. It is a long and tedious exercise.

When he finishes asking her questions, he makes additional notes and says, "We will start again."

During the second round of questioning, Jason interjects a story about his troubled son and the difficulty he was having in school. Kim wonders why he is telling her the story. She sympathizes.

Then he adds, "Only through the efforts of his new teacher, is he showing progress. It is like she lifted a fog from his brain; he's doing okay and expected to go to college."

"That's wonderful," Kim responds, a little puzzled about why the story is being told until…

"She's a Jewish lady," Jason conveys.

There it is! He checks the machine. Kim is almost amused at his graceless attempt to determine her religion.

After the test is over and he informs her she passed, she inquires, "If you want to know my religion, why don't you ask?"

Of course, they both know, by law he is not allowed to, but she challenges him anyway; It is a sneaky thing to do and she is no longer amused.

As Jason unhooks her and packs up his machine, he explains, "I was raised in a small town like Mayberry in the old Andy Griffith television show in a part of the country where there were no Jews and up until recently, I had never met one until my son's teacher."

"And?" Kim urged.

"Well, I am astounded to meet another one, particularly a woman in an Arizona police department."

Not quite an apology. Kim is surprised by his lack of sophistication and wonders if he has a white sheet in hidden in his briefcase.

11

Kim, the Volunteer

It's Kim's first day at the station. Jack introduces her to the staff.

"Before we put you to work, I want to apologize for Jason's behavior. He told me what happened," Jack said.

"I've experienced this before. Ignorance and arrogance are a dangerous combination," Kim states with a mixture of disappointment and well-worn tolerance.

"I agree, "It won't happen again, I promise." Jack assures her. "Now, let's get you to Alice."

Alice is a sweet lady, tall, heavyset and single. She's in her forties, lives with her grandmother and five parrots and talks incessantly about movie stars. She reads all the gossip publications, attends movies every Friday and in her spare time, writes fan letters and collects Hollywood memorabilia. She doesn't have many friends, one or two from school with whom she spends time occasionally, but she is liked by all in the department.

Alice's focus is on her growing collection and insists their value will skyrocket by the time she is ready to retire. And that is her retirement plan. Her intention is to collect as many autographs of the rich and famous as she can so that when she is ready to sell, they will provide her with a healthy income. She is obsessed with Tom Cruise and fantasizes often what life would be like in his arms. Alice is a paid civilian in charge of the Pawn Detail.

By law, pawn brokers have to complete a form each time they accept an item in exchange for a monetary loan. The item has to be pre-owned, not stolen and is kept on file with the police department. Kim's first assignment is to collect the forms, organize them by date, and shop and prepare a summary sheet for Alice. Reports will then be sent to local police departments.

Alice brings Kim a glass of water and a can of soda. "Thank you but I didn't request anything to drink."

"I need to keep you moist," Alice cackles.

"Why?" Kim inquires, almost afraid of the answer.

Alice hands Kim a box of letters and replies. "All of these letters need to be sealed."

Kim burst into laughter and excused herself. She went to the ladies' room and found a sponge in the cabinet underneath the sink. She returned to her desk and asked, "Alice, did you really expect me to lick over a hundred envelopes? Is that what you do with one can of soda and one cup of water?" Alice is baffled. "Doesn't everybody?"

The following week, Kim brought in a sponge from an office supply store.

Jack visits the precinct often. From time to time he and Kim have lunch with other volunteers or staff and Jack regales them with his stories of dumb criminals like the guy who tried to collect the reward for his own capture by bringing in his wanted poster to the local police station and demanding the money. Those times are fun and informative. Kim enjoys hearing about crimes from those directly in charge of solving them. She has great respect for law enforcement officers and what they endure.

Jack is always a perfect gentleman around her, but she is not unaware of his attraction toward her. She simply does not feel the same. She limits their time alone and keeps things on a friendly business basis.

The precinct is in a low-crime area. The worst crimes are the theft of mountain bikes, golf clubs and horse riding equipment stolen from open garages. There are many ranches and horse properties as well as a buffalo ranch located in the small town.

Most of the police officers served in the military, all are in excellent shape and train hard in the desert. One of the exercises requires them to run up and down the mountains with forty pounds of weight on their backs. Their motto is, "If you're not sworn, you're not born." Practically everyone carries a gun. Brad and Kim feel quite safe in their new environment

12

The Investigation

The Cadillac DeVille case is ongoing. The decimated building
housed eight small businesses owned by an accountant, a mail order
operation, a computer repair shop, an insurance agency, a maintenance
company, a clothing rep, a real estate office and a temp agency for
office workers. The people who ran those small businesses had to find
new office space and try to reconstruct their files and records, most
of which were lost in the blast. Insurance reps combed the site for
months, taking photos and preparing reports. The landlord settled
with his insurance company and left the state after being cleared of
any wrongdoing.

Enough of the dead guy was found to identify him, three fingers
and a broken partial bridge with a few teeth were strewn about in
the front seat of the Cadillac. The car was easy to trace via the vin
number. The dead guy was Willie Falcone, aka Wille the Weasel.

Shortly after testifying against his bosses in New York, Willie the
Weasel was given a new identity and relocated to Arizona where he
was in the witness protection program. The poor sap worked for the
maintenance company and had just finished his shift cleaning the
building when the blast occurred. Amongst the remains, we found
his maintenance report and check out time. He was probably on his
way home.

Willie was well known to local police; he ran an illegal gambling
ring out of his apartment. And he was a local celebrity of sorts.

Willie, a professional gambler was a natural born salesman. Small
and stick-thin in stature, with a thick head of black curly hair and

frisbee sized black eyes, he was a memorable character totally out of place in a quiet little western town. He was highly energetic, moved like a rabbit, talked fast and loud and invariably had a joke to share. He ended most sentences with, *Ratatatat, know what I mean?* He was an upbeat guy, always ready to party. He loved the criminal life and would sell his first born to place a bet.

Within days we checked his small one bedroom apartment in Phoenix. It was filthy.

In the kitchen, dirty dishes were in the sink and on every surface. Old, decaying fast food in various containers dotted the counters and overflowed the garbage can. Food containers of various sizes and contents were found in every room including the bathroom.

The only furniture in the living room was a card table covered with decks of cards, plastic colored chips and ashtrays filled with the residue of cigarettes and cigars. In the bedroom we found typewriter supplies; but no typewriter, files, notebooks or receipts. Dirty laundry was piled in a corner next to the unmade bed. Tucked in amongst the laundry pile were cassette tapes which would prove to be quite valuable to investigators later on in identifying Willie's playmates. Willie recorded all conversations during card games, over the telephone and in person meetings. Willie kept records. Where were they?

Despite the sloppy way Willie lived, we could tell the place had been ransacked. Every drawer, cabinet and closet had been opened and disturbed. There were empty shoe boxes with remnants of bank wrappers. Whatever cash he had was long gone. We had the apartment cordoned off and dusted for fingerprints. He had an interesting group of visitors which included a couple of low-level criminals with long records. One set of prints was apparently lost in the system. Now we had to find out who wanted him dead and why?

Bored in exile, Willie openly bragged about his criminal activities to anyone who would listen. During this time, there was talk about bringing Vegas-style gambling to Arizona and turning some of the high end resorts into casinos. The timing was perfect for Willie. Ever the entrepreneur, he approached a local television show producer and pitched an idea for a segment on "How to be a Shrewd Gambler,"

The producer came down to the station and filled us in on Willie's star status. Willie promised to educate the public about the risks and triumphs of what he called 'Shrewd Gambling' whether it was with card games, sports betting or horse racing. He actually presented the producer with a smart and thoughtful common sense outline on the do's and don'ts of Shrewd Gambling. The plan was to educate the audience about the rules of the games and help them avoid losing their mortgage money or taking food out of their children's mouths. In other words, to prevent them from forming an addiction to gambling. Willie saw his contribution as his civic duty.

The producer gave us Willie's typed list:

The Dos and Don'ts of Shrewd Gambling by Willie Falcone

Do have plan.

Don't waiver from that plan

Do choose an area of interest (cards, sports, horse racing)

Don't bet on everything that comes across your path

Do know the rules of the game

Don't break the rules

Do set an amount of money to invest in gambling

Don't go beyond the set amount

Do plan for wins

Don't spend beyond the wins

Do plan for losses

Don't feed the losses

Do gamble with confidence

Don't gamble in an impaired state (alcohol, drugs, exhaustion or illness)

An enterprising but naive young reporter was assigned to interview Willie on a live broadcast about the life of a professional gambler and, unintentionally, made them both local celebrities. The people at the television station were unaware that Willie was in a witness protection program. However, at his request they agreed that to protect Willie's privacy as a professional gambler, they would allow him to appear behind a screen with his voice distorted during the interview. Willie was given a script containing a series of general questions about gambling based on his list of do's and don'ts, He was asked to prepare brief, easy to understand responses for a curious public.

During the live interview, Willie strayed off topic and bragged that he could smell a gangster a mile away. He boasted that he befriended everyone he met. A party guy, he talked about collecting a list of names and contact information of other criminal colleagues. Willie gloated about the fact that he started a private club called Killers, Gamblers and Thieves (KIGATHS). He gleefully announced the fact that he had t-shirts made up and charged his cohorts five dollars apiece.

Mesmerized by the information Willie was eager to impart about his sordid criminal past, the interviewer let Willie ramble on off topic instead of taking control of the interview. When It was over, Willie earned a standing ovation from the television audience. He glowed in the attention.

Everyone I knew listened to the interview-law enforcement officers did so for authenticity and clues to crimes. Everyone else for gossip, something to discuss around the water cooler the following day. What is it about criminals that excites the law abiding public so much? Particularly, mob related stories. Doesn't the public understand that these are bad guys?

The station was flooded with calls. Willie was an instant success. The public wanted more interviews with Willie and sent in money to purchase t-shirts. The station was glad to comply with additionally scheduled interviews but smartly declined to sell the t-shirts and refunded all the money received. Willie was booked for a series of interviews which went national and were later broadcast on the radio as well.

13

Kim's New Volunteer Assignment

A former New York detective introduces himself to Kim and invites her to lunch. Miguel Acevedo is in his mid-forties, powerfully built, not an ounce of fat on his lean six foot frame. His soft black hair flops to one side. He constantly brushes it away from his green eyes. He reminds Kim of a 1960's rock star.

Miguel is in charge of the gang unit and explains to Kim that gangs are recruiting kids through school as young as eight or nine years old. Kim is horrified to hear that and agrees to help in any way she can.

Kim's job is to enter photos of gang members, their tattoos and written statements describing various crimes into a secure computer in a locked location with glass windows on three sides.

In that room is the hotline phone and from time to time, investigating officers listen to evidence tapes at the opposite end of the room from where Kim works. One day, she arrives to make her entries; her presence ignored by three officers gathered around a tape machine as she goes to the far side of the room to work on the secure computer.

She hears snippets of a conversation among a group of men, maybe five who appeared to be playing cards at the home of someone named Willie. He has a most interesting speech pattern and ends most sentences with *"Ratatatat, know what I mean?"* He and his friends talk about the old days, their criminal activities and how they got into the life.

34

There is another tape which apparently provides proof in an open case. The officers listen to it several times; the tapes are of poor quality and spotty.

"Willie! You're a star."

"You saw me on TV?"

"I did."

"I didn't mention any names, right? Just teased the audience a bit. Right? *Ratatatat, you know what I mean?*

"Yeah, Willie. I know what you mean."

"You're not mad or anything are ya', Johnny?"

"I told ya, call me Harry."

"Harry, yeah yeah I'm sorry Harry. I really didn't mean anything by it. You're not mad, right?"

"Nah. "

"Good. Because this is my ticket to Hollywood."

"Hollywood?"

"Yeah, my dream of being in the movies. *Ratatatat, you know what I mean?*"

"Yeah, sure. I know what you mean. Listen, I need a favor."

"Sure, sure Harry, whaddya need?"

"A ride in your shiny new Cadillac."

"That's easy. Where we goin'?"

"Out to an abandoned mine shaft. There's construction around there and I gotta pick up some dynamite."

"You gonna rob a bank?"

"You'll be the first to know. Meet me at the casino tomorrow morning about 7:00 a.m. It's a long ride."

The officers are particularly interested in that tape. That is all she hears. Is the voice familiar? She ignores the tapes. She has plenty of data to enter.

Kim finishes her entries and prepares a summary for Miguel. He is in the process of meeting with parents' and teachers' groups to educate them about the growing gang problem and is eager to present his reports to them. He is frustrated by the fact that many parents and teachers refuse to believe gangs exist and are a growing threat in the schools. He is concerned about an escalating situation being ignored. He works directly with the kids he arrests. He is a good guy trying to set those kids straight. He is receiving little support from the community.

Kim and Miguel form a strong working relationship. He asks her to serve on a committee which awards grants to community programs serving at-risk youth and they travel together to visit the programs and attend council meetings. There is great pride and satisfaction in the work. Miguel nominates Kim for special recognition in the precinct.

One day over lunch, Miguel confesses a long held secret to her. As a teen, he had hung out with a bunch of guys in a gang in uptown Manhattan and wasn't proud of it. They committed petty crimes and misdemeanors and generally caused havoc in the neighborhood. They played a dangerous game. They jumped the turnstiles without paying their fare to get into the subways, both elevated and underground. Then they spent hours daring each other to run from side to side across the tracks in front of oncoming trains. No one got hurt, but one day, Miguel slipped and caught his foot in the track. The train barreled down on him and at the last minute he was able to pull his foot out of his sneaker. What was left of the sneaker disintegrated. He hobbled home with one sneaker, terrified to tell his folks what happened.

The next day he went to confession. The priest made clear that he had been saved so that he could save others. That day, he decided that instead of committing crimes, he would prevent them. He focused on his education, became a police officer and worked his way up through the ranks.

When Kim begins her work in the gang unit, the gang kids are stealing cigarettes and beer for the older boys as an initiation process. Eventually, the gang unit is absorbed by the violent crimes division.

Miguel is correct. The gangs are running rampant and out of control. Miguel eventually leaves the precinct. Kim never knows why, nor does she ever speak with him again. Kim's work in the gang unit is eventually taken over by a paid civilian. She is ready for her next assignment.

14

Willie the Weasel --A Rising Star

The Boss sits behind his large heavy dark mahogany desk. Although burdened by being born into generations of criminal leaders, he is respected by his crew and the heads of competing families. He is a smart and fair businessman and treats his underlings well, making sure they all have enough money to support their families. He does everything expected of him but what he really wants to do is be an electronic engineer.

He treasures his IBM computer which has a Pentium microprocessor. Computers are becoming faster but still reliant on a MS-DOS (Microsoft Disk Operating System.) Separate telephone lines are required for a dial up a connection.

The Boss wants to modernize his home office and make sure the people who work for him are up on the latest technology. It is difficult because while the female office staff members catch on easily, the male crew members have trouble. Half of them never finished grade school. How do you teach uneducated guys technology? Games. Once they master Doom 1, he teaches them email. He makes sure that each crew member has the latest computer that the market will bear or whatever falls off the delivery truck.

The Boss and his crew sit and watch television often.

One day they focus on a naïve young talk show host interviewing a man in disguise behind a screen whose voice has been altered.

The host concludes "So then you are saying there is a strict code of silence in your world, am I right?"

"You betcha! *Ratatatat, know what I mean?*" laughs the guest.

"What happens if someone breaks that code?" The host asks innocently.

"He ends up as part of some landfill or at the bottom of a river." The man mumbled his answer.

"The host pressed on. So, terms like "cement shoes" and "sleeping with the fishes" are true?"

The man laughed as did the audience. "Yes, little boy. It happens. You can read about it every day in the New York Post."

"Are you from New York?"

"I'm from everywhere and I know everybody. I can tell you stories about people who rip off the public in ways you'd never suspect."

"Boss, that's Willie, we found Willie! How do you like that? The little weasel wound up in Phoenix and on television!" Carl Mitchello cries. Carl is all muscle, not too bright in the head but young, loyal and dependable. He takes care of his body and parades it in tight black t-shirts and black slacks and he always wears dark sunglasses, even at night. He just thinks it makes him look cool. The Boss treats him like he was his own son.

The Boss is unhappy. "Goddam it, Willie, you talk too damned much!" The Boss is worried. "Listen, Carl, this is what I want you to do. Go to Phoenix on the next flight, find the weasel and shut him up for good. He knows too much and has already cost me a lot of money."

"I'm on it!" Carl gleefully replies.

15

Willie the Weasel --A Falling Star

John Banion, aka Harry Gellis, is in the witness protection program also located in Arizona. Why? He is married to Rosa DeBola the daughter of a man murdered by his own brother on a quest for power. Rosa is arrested for money laundering and turns state's evidence. Her testimony is backed up by John who has convictions for burglary, manslaughter and rape. She and John testify against her uncle and other family members and reveal family secrets that put her uncle, several family members and many of her uncle's companions in prison.

Although Rosa is much younger than John, she dies soon after relocating to Arizona leaving John a widower with a big bounty on his head. John quickly morphs into the lonely widower Harry Gellis.

Harry Gellis is a large man, about 6'2", broad shouldered and powerfully strong for his age – late seventies. He wears a thick gold chain around his neck, his shirt open to mid chest, collar flipped up. He is a bully with a combustible temper, no social graces but fancies himself a ladies' man and often makes crude remarks and weak attempts at humor.

Harry, with cigarette in one hand, slouches on his torn recliner next to a table covered with sleazy girlie magazines, over-flowing ashtrays and the remnants of a TV dinner while he watches television.

He focuses on a naïve young talk show host interviewing a man in disguise behind a screen whose voice has been altered.

The host concludes "So then you are saying there is a strict code of silence in your world, am I right?"

"You betcha! *Ratatatat, know what I mean?*" laughs the guest.

"What happens if someone breaks that code?" The host asks innocently.

"He ends up as part of some landfill or at the bottom of a river." The man mumbles his answer.

"The host presses on. So, terms like "cement shoes" and "sleeping with the fishes" are true?"

The man laughs now as does the audience. "Yes, little boy. It happens. You can read about it every day in the New York Post."

"Are you from New York?"

"I'm from everywhere and I know everybody. Why I can tell you stories about people who rip off the public in ways you'd never suspect. Not only that, but you got a heavy hitter hiding right here in your quiet little town as a guest of the taxpayers. *Ratatatat know what I mean?*"

"Actually, I don't. Let's go to commercial and when we return, we will talk about common sense rules everyone should know about shrewd gambling whether you're playing cards, betting on horse races or sports. Stay tuned."

Harry shuts off the television. "Willie, Willie, you talk too damned much! He yells at the TV. It's unfortunate you saw me at the casino. I just wanted a nice little poker game to offset the boredom and now you're going to tell everyone where I am. Tsk, tsk, tsk. Not too smart Willie, not smart at all!"

Harry paces around the living room, his anger rolling forward. He finally screams, "You, asshole!" and throws his dinner at the television. He flops back down into his favorite chair and ponders his next move. He searches through newspapers until he finds what he is looking for and rereads the article several times. He has a plan; he relaxes and dials his phone. Willie answers.

"Willie; You're a star."

"You saw me on TV?"

"I did."

"I didn't mention any names, right? Just teased the audience a bit. Right? *Ratatatat, you know what I mean?*"

"Yeah, Willie. I know what you mean."

"You're not mad or anything are ya', Johnny?"

"I told ya, call me Harry."

"Harry, yeah yeah I'm sorry Harry. I really didn't mean anything by it. You're not mad, right?"

"Nah. "

"Good. Because this is my ticket to Hollywood."

"Hollywood?"

"Yeah, my dream of being in the movies. *Ratatatat, you know what I mean?*"

"Yeah, sure. I know what you mean. Listen, I need a favor."

"Sure, sure Harry, whaddya need?"

"A ride in your shiny new Cadillac."

"That's easy. Where we goin'?"

"Out to an abandoned mine shaft. There's construction around there and I gotta pick up some dynamite."

"You gonna rob a bank?"

"You'll be the first to know. Meet me at the casino tomorrow morning about 7:00 a.m. It's a long ride."

Seven o'clock in the morning, Willie is in front of the casino. Harry barrels out the door, slams it shut and gets into the car. He has a canvas bag filled with bubble wrap and maps in his hands.

"I bought ya' coffee, Where we goin'?" Willie hands Harry a cup of coffee.

"Get on I-17 going north, I'll tell ya' from there."

Harry sips the coffee. "Whaddya put in here?"

"Just those creamer things – two of them and a couple of sugars, just like you like it."

"Ugh" Harry spits the coffee out the window and tosses the container after it just missing a pedestrian. "Get goin'."

"Anything you say, Johnny." He slaps his head. "I mean Harry."

After a few minutes of silence, Willie says, "I'm sure glad I ran into you at the casino."

"Yeah, My lucky day."

Willie isn't sure if Harry is being earnest or sarcastic. He shrugs it off.

"I hate it out here. What about you, Harry?"

"I know what you mean. No one to talk to. Everything is so dry, especially the people. No sense of humor."

"Yeah, there's nothin' like Brooklyn where there's always somethin' going on." He pauses wistfully. "But we can never go back."

"So, you go someplace else, like Mexico."

"We can't. They keep a close eye on us. Besides which, it ain't so bad. *Ratatatat, know what I mean?*"

"You having fun, Willie?"

"Yeah. Do you believe it, they want me back on television! Do you think I need an agent or somethin'?"

"Maybe. You're a big TV star now, Willie. We just have to figure out whether your risin' or fallin'."

"Good one, Harry. Good one."

"Stop at the next gas station. I gotta go."

"Sure, Harry, sure."

Harry studies his maps. Willie drives in silence until he pulls into a gas station.

Willie exits the car. "I think my ass fell asleep. I'm gonna walk around and stretch my bones."

"Yeah, you do that and buy some sandwiches or something. We got a ways to go."

"Sure, Harry, Sure."

While Harry is in the men's room, Willie changes the tape on his little recorder, then proceeds to buy sandwiches and snacks for the rest of the trip.

Within two hours, they arrive at a closed construction site near an old abandoned silver mine.

"How'd you know about this place?" Willie asks.

"There is a story about it in the local newspaper with pictures."

"How do ya' know where the dynamite is?"

Harry points to a fenced in area with a big sign that reads "Caution Explosives"

"Do you know how to handle dynamite?"

"How hard could it be?"

"Well, just be careful. This is a brand new car. *Ratatatat, know what I mean?*"

"Don't worry about it. You just drive."

By three o'clock in the afternoon Willie drops Harry and his bag full of dynamite at the casino.

In subsequent television interviews, Willie goes too far. He gloats not only about his own criminal past, but also teases the audience with the tidbit that he knows the whereabouts of a significant player in the indictment against major criminal figures. That morsel seals his fate.

Willie just talks too much. Suddenly, my quiet little town becomes a vacation destination for Willie's old friends. My buddies tell me that after several months of investigation and even with the help of Willie's hidden laundry tapes, they still don't have enough information to make an arrest. The case remains open but inactive.

16

Jack's Pima Vista Retirement Village Work Buddies

After retirement, I have more quality time to spend with my friends. There is a group of guys I hang out with once a month or so. Most of them work in a new retirement community called Pima Vista Retirement Village.

I was invited into the group by Randi Loughman, a golf buddy. Randi is about fifty, ex-military, strong and dependable. He is always dressed in perfectly pressed jeans, crisp white shirt and spit-shined shoes. He openly carries a 40 Caliber Glock 22 and constantly chews gum to prevent him from smoking. His blond hair tinged with white cut short military style frames clear steely brown eyes and a strong jaw. His determined manner inspires thoughts of a comic book hero.

Randi is a man's man but not very tolerant of nor respectful towards women. He questions their intelligence, enjoys bedding them, but he is of the strong opinion that they have their place in society and it is solely in the home. Randy is single, never married. At least, I tried. Randi is the property manager at Pima Vista.

Sean Mason is an angry sonofabitch, a misguided patriot. He spends his time judging everyone and complaining about everything, particularly politicians who according to him are "sending us into oblivion." With his strong opinions and lack of filters, he just isn't very good with people in social situations. Also, ex-military, he is built like a tank, wide and powerful. The guy is a beast. Shaking hands with him feels like an arm-wrestle. His brown crewcut does not flatter his moon face and beady distrusting grey eyes. He favors camouflage clothes and loves wood and weapons. Still in his thirties, he is on his second divorce and trolling the bars for company.

Sean is a master craftsman. He is highly skilled and proficient at fixing anything; plumbing, electrical you name it. He can build any structure from a rough sketch. Heck, he even built his own trailer home. He has the tools and the knowhow. He does good work at Pima Vista. Sean is the maintenance guy at Pima Vista.

Phil Capshaw is in his forties. A little overweight slightly balding with pock-marked sallow skin, he wears Buddy Holly glasses over his dull tired eyes. Somehow, no matter how many times he showers, he never looks clean. He sweats profusely and always seems to have a five o'clock shadow and deep, dark bags under his eyes. He reminds me of a pile of soiled laundry. Phil claims to love women, all women except his wife. He is unhappily married to a hoarder who collects everything including broken dolls, vintage clothing, remnants of fabric, old newspapers bottles…It drives him nuts. He prefers to hang out with the guys rather than spend time at home. He admires Randi's confidence, Sean's skills and my career. He has no joy in his life.

Phil had been a long distance trucker before coming to work at Pima Vista. He has a vast knowledge about the roads of America, coast to coast and always has a story to tell about the goings on at the truck stops. Insecure and a bit of a whiner, he is courteous and capable at work. Phil is the shuttle driver at Pima Vista.

We all live within a few miles of each other and agree to meet at a designated house before our nights out, which usually means burgers and bars. I serve cheese, crackers and nuts, beer, wine and soda. Sean, the angry master craftsman is a chips, dips, pretzel and beer guy. Randi the property manager who disrespects women serves microwaved frozen hors d'oeuvres. The first time when it was Phil the driver's turn, it was an embarrassing disaster. I drove Sean and

Randi to the address Phil gave us. There was so much debris in the front yard, a fire hazard to be sure, we thought it was an abandoned property and we had the wrong address.

We were about to leave when the door creaked open and a toothless, barefoot overweight forties something woman in a torn house dress motioned to us mumbling, "Follow me." She led us in single file through narrow pathways past haphazardly stored clutter. Furniture, piles of clothing, boxes stacked to the ceiling; it was mind-boggling. She stopped, looked us all up and down pointed to a bridge table with four plastic chairs and disappeared into the morass. Space was tight, we could hardly move and jockeyed for our respective places. I'm not afraid of the dark, nor do I jump at noises in the night, but I was feeling anxious about what may have been lurking under the filthy piles of crap. Phil appeared from what seemed to be the back of the house and gave us each a can of soda. There was no room on the table for cups or straws. It was awkward. We left early for the bar.

17

Kim and Brad Buy a House

After a few months, Kim turns fifty. She and Brad decide it is time to see their dream of owning a home come to life. She has never lived in a house, just apartments from the time she was born in Brooklyn through her adult years spent in Manhattan. Brad is nervous because of her bleak future but she remains optimistic and wants to experience a home and make sure he has a comfortable place to live--in case.

Brad turns over the project to Kim who happily contacts a local real estate broker named Lance. Lance, a transplant from California who gave up a not-so-promising acting career is a trophy-winning body builder, semi-bald with radiant aqua-colored eyes. He has a wicked sense of humor, an abundance of patience and would soon become the number one real estate agent in the area. His ebullience is infectious, and he and Kim have a fun time searching for a new home in different neighborhoods outside of Phoenix.

The majority of the homes Lance shows her are established which means, the need for a remodel to upgrade appliances, electric, plumbing and sewer systems. Most of them need painting inside and out, roof, driveway and pool repairs. Neither Kim nor Brad have the skill, knowledge and perhaps the time, so she asks if there are any new builds within their budget.

Lance promises he will do a search and finds a gem. Pima Vista Retirement Village, a mixed-use complex consisting of newly-built private homes and a shopping center side by side hidden in the back roads off a major roadway. It is charming, right in the heart of Scottsdale, quaint, affordable and less than a mile from a major hospital. It's perfect!

Kim urges Brad to join her and Lance the following Sunday to see it. As soon as they walk into the model, they both feel uplifted. The sales agent is kind, courteous and eager to please. There are only five lots left. Kim and Brad make their decision and leave a good faith deposit that day.

In celebration, they visit the shopping center and have a pleasant lunch in one of the five restaurants all within walking distance. They shop in the clothing store and make note of the bank, the cleaners, the hairdresser and most importantly, the supermarket with a pharmacy attached. Perfect! Walkable and convenient. If it were too hot to walk or if Kim wasn't feeling strong enough, the Pima Vista Shuttle makes the rounds to and from the shopping area on a scheduled basis.

Within the week, they meet the construction supervisor at Pima Vista Retirement Village, Lennard Jayko. Lennard Jayko, thirty-five, an educated Pima Indian is a nice guy, efficient and quiet. Everything about him is quiet, his demeanor, his movements, his voice. No one knows much about him except that he does good work, is reliable and devoted to his mother. He is tall, neatly groomed and always wears blue shirts with his tight jeans.

Lennard leads them through the building process and explains every phase of construction. They are promised their home will be completed within six months. The timing is perfect. Construction begins immediately, takes place seven days a week and is completed a month earlier than promised. It is a joy to see the structure built from the ground up on a vacant lot.

During visits to and from their sprouting home, Kim and Brad plan for their future. Brad is happier, Kim is adjusting to her physical challenges, and they share a renewed cheerful spirit.

18

Lennard Jayko Becomes A Friend

Kim spends a lot of time with Lennard as the construction progresses and they have many opportunities to share stories about their different backgrounds. His dream is to visit New York and they talk endlessly about Manhattan, it's energy and value as one of the greatest cities in the world.

He is eager to visit the United Nations Building, see the Statue of Liberty, spend time on Broadway, stroll through Central Park, ride the subway and taste the hot dogs and pretzels from street vendors. She is amazed at his knowledge of life in New York City, that which perhaps she has taken for granted.

Lennard, a Pima Indian is a member of one of the local Indian communities in the county. Kim has been reading about the various tribes in Arizona and started alphabetically with the Ak-Chin Indian Community in Pinal County with the intention of covering all the tribes up to the Zuni Heaven Reservation in Apache County. The reservations cover almost a quarter of the land in Arizona.

Lennard reminds her that history was written through white eyes. He isn't angry about the past and is pleased to share stories about daily life in the desert, the traditions and beliefs of his culture and graciously answers any questions she has.

Brad and Kim often visit the Heard Museum which has marvelous collections of artifacts, photographic history and often hosts ceremonial dance recitals performed by Native American adults and children. Sadly, the Buffalo Museum shut its doors, but it too, was a center of invaluable information.

19
Moving Day

Finally, it is moving day! Lennard and Sean stand next to a maintenance truck with "Pima Vista Retirement Village" painted on the side.

They watch as three landscapers secure a saguaro cactus.

Sean is pleased and declares, "Another house sold. We're doin' good, huh?"

"Not good enough," states Lennard. "We have 12 units to sell in this section and more over in the west end.

"Well, I don't want to get laid off again, you hear me dude?"

Kim and Brad follow their moving truck and park in their new driveway. Lennard notices them.

"Better get those grab bars going," he orders Sean.

Sean moves at a snail's pace towards the maintenance truck and mumbles, "I don't need you to tell me my job."

Brad and Kim exit their car and are immediately mesmerized by the sight. It is simply stunning. She leans on Brad and just stands mute, gazing at their home. It is their first house and to them it is a castle. They are so proud and engrossed in all the activity that they leave the engine running and the car doors open.

"Isn't that majestic?" Kim loves cacti and marvels at the fact that so many species grow throughout the desert without care and feeding. They represent an independent strength which inspires her, and she plans on having several species around their home.

Brad jokes that Arizona landscaping is practically maintenance-free, river rock, a boulder and cacti.

Lennard approaches. "You left your engine running."

Brad hurries back to the car, shuts the engine down and closes the doors.

"You folks from the east need to slow down and enjoy the view."

He is right. They need to slow down, and the view is spectacular! Life is slower in Arizona and it takes some getting used to. That morning Kim stood in line at the grocery store. Used to being rushed through lines in Manhattan, she is amazed while the cashier and the customer in front of her chat about their children and which ones like vegetables and which ones don't and she wants to scream, "Move, who cares?"

She doesn't, of course and realizes she is in a friendly place and people care about each other and take the time to get to know one another. She listens patiently and is invited into the conversation. It is pleasant, reminds her of her humanity and at that moment, she feels her healing begins.

Brad and she watch as three muscular movers in their twenties work in sync unloading furniture and belongings swiftly and carefully in the heat; the stifling heat!

"How do you like the finished product?" Lennard inquires.

"Perfect!" they say in unison.

Lennard hands Brad the keys. In a burst of enthusiasm, Brad lifts Kim off the ground and carries her over the threshold. She runs her fingers through Brad's beautiful salt and pepper hair and kisses him gently on the cheek.

They hear a collective "Awww."

The movers follow them in. All work stops as they are greeted with applause. It is a joyful moment. So far everyone is most welcoming.

Brad places her down on their new carpet and whispers, "Home sweet home, sweetie."

They kiss again. "You are so romantic," she sighs.

Lennard brings their luggage in and the work begins. Kim removes color coded tags from her purse and pastes them on various doorways. The movers follow her around placing boxes with matching color codes in each room.

Space! They finally have room to spread out. They are thrilled by bathrooms larger than telephone booths and bedrooms, three of them plus a den which she has plans to turn into a working office. They have vaulted ceilings, bay windows and there is a feeling of great space, an unattainable premium in New York for them. Now, they have a fireplace, a jetted tub, a yard with a swimming pool and quiet. The only sounds they hear are birds chirping in the backyard.

Brad is in a state of euphoria. "This is paradise."

"Are all the handicapped adjustments complete?" Brad asks.

Lennard checks his list. "Slide out drawers, tilted mirrors and Sean is installing grab bars in the second bathroom."

A mover enters with a metal bath chair and Brad directs him to the master bathroom.

It is a happy chaos with the movers deftly manipulating furniture and boxes while Brad and Lennard stroll through the house for a last walk through. Sean checks all the electrical and plumbing.

Kim moves to the kitchen area and sits on a chair one of the men brings in, her cane at her side. Just then, the doorbell rings. Before anyone has a chance to respond, Pat Wilson, about sixty-five, barges through the open door carrying a large basket which partially hides her face. Her wide-brimmed pastel colored floral designed hat, blocks the rest of her facial features except for her burning brown eyes.

"Helloooo. I am your Welcome Wagon Lady. My name is Pat. I'm known as Pat in the Hat! I collect hats you see."

Kim stands to greet her and leans on her cane. She is mesmerized as Pat models her aqua, pink and mint green hat, twirling and bowing, basket in hand. Her wide-collared pink blouse is neatly tucked into her flowing pastel colored floral designed skirt which dances in the breeze she creates. She is lithe, slightly hunched probably from arthritis or osteoporosis but quick on her flip-flop covered feet with energy to burn.

Kim has a good look at Pat as she clings to the basket. Under the wide-brimmed hat, she wears far too much makeup. Her eye shadow is smeared, her thick black eye liner is formed in a cat eye style and her mascara is too thick, it looks like it is caked from several days' usage. Her teased, dried and brittle hair is dyed ruby red and her pink orange rouge is applied in a wide circle under her eyes, rivaling her bright orange lipstick.

Brad hurries into the room when he hears the commotion and stands at Kim's side. Pat looks them up and down before she continues. "Soooo, you're Brad and Kim from the Big Apple."

"Yes," they answer in unison.

Pat turns to Brad and says "Aren't you handsome. Do you know what they call a handsome man at Pima Vista Retirement Village?" Without waiting for an answer, she laughs and says, "A guest."

Brad and Kim come to the same conclusion. Pat is single.

In the midst of all the confusion, without stopping to catch her breath, Pat prattles on and has their attention. Maybe they are taking a break. Maybe they want to know more about this woman.

"So," she continues, "I hear you are in sales. Any discounts for friendly neighbors?"

Kim remains silent. She's not liking Pat's aggressive manner.

Brad gently responds, "I'm in the antique and collectibles business with an emphasis on vintage watches."

"Well that sounds rather dull," she retorts.

Now Kim is amused by her lack of filters.

Pat quickly turns to Kim, "So, Kim, now that you are retired, I'm sure you will enjoy all our amenities. In fact, I know you'll love our fantastic new library. It's open seven days a week!"

"I'm sure I will. I get my information from the Internet. Tell me, where do you get yours?"

Coyly Pat teases, "Ooooh a little birdie." And as an aside, she whispers, "Her name is Jennifer and she works in the office. I bring her two muffins every week and she tells me all the gossip around here, who moves in, who moves out."

Kim makes a mental note to speak to Jennifer.

"Oops, I nearly forgot why I'm here! Welcome to Pima Vista Retirement Village!" Pat shouts and rams the basket into Kim's hands. Kim's cane crashes onto the new marble floor. Pat does not acknowledge it nor offer to pick it up. Brad to the rescue. "I'll take that."

He knows the basket is too heavy for Kim. As he places it on the counter and retrieves her cane, Pat pirouettes and inspects their furniture as if it is a crime scene. "Oooh, nice furniture!"

She proceeds to flit through the house from room to room. Kim is feeling displeased. She looks at Brad. He takes the cue. Brad follows Pat and guides her back to the kitchen where Kim sits and says, "We thank you for the basket."

"What?" It is obvious to them Pat is distracted by her own need to snoop. Then she does something odd. She walks to a blank wall and stares at it for several seconds as if in a trance.

"Tell us what's in the basket," Brad gently prompts. He has to repeat himself.

She snaps to attention and rambles on, "The basket has maps, coupons, the Smile-A-Ride Shuttle schedule and a special surprise."

Brad plows through the basket, removes the shuttle schedule and remarks, "Oh, good, Kim can use the shuttle while I am at work."

Pat waits. "Did you find my surprise yet?"

She has a sweet smile, child-like. Kim begins to feel less angry at her behavior.

Brad acts like a kid when he finds a paper plate covered in saran wrap. "Cookies!" he declares.

Proudly, Pat announces, "'Baked them myself from scratch. You see, I'm taking a culinary arts cooking class. Tonight, it's Italian; gotta go grate the gorgonzola. Ciaooo."

She waves her hand as if she is royalty, whirls around like a tornado, heads towards the door and is gone. Kim decides she has a good heart and might be a fun neighbor, but she is concerned about

Pat's momentary trance.

Kim and Brad are hungry, so they munch on the cookies which are delicious and leave the remaining cookies on the counter for the movers, Lennard and Sean. Lennard takes a cookie; Sean takes a handful.

"Great cookies," Brad exclaims in between bites.

"She's a good neighbor," Lennard offers.

"And well informed," Kim adds.

Pat pops back into the house. "I'm also your crime watch captain. If you need anything, I am across the street. You can't miss me. I wear the most interesting hats. Bye, bye."

Poof! Like magic, she disappears.

After several hours, the movers leave. Brad pays them and includes tips for each.

As Lennard comes into the kitchen, Brad gives him $50.00 and says simply, "Thank you. We couldn't have done this without you. Everything is perfect."

Sean watches the transaction from the hallway. He is angry.

Lennard says, "Mr. Wolf, I was just doing my job. It isn't necessary, really."

"We'd both feel better if you accepted it," Brad answers.

"In that case, I will." Lennard removes an envelope from his pocket and scribbles something on it. Neither Brad nor Kim can tell what he wrote.

Sean leaves in haste and slams the door. Lennard apologizes for him. Brad and Kim forgive Sean's behavior agreeing he is probably tired. They all are. Brad excuses himself and begins to unpack in the back rooms.

Kim needs a breath of fresh air, so she accompanies Lennard as he leaves for the day. They say their good-byes and as they stand by the mailbox, the wind picks up. Dark clouds cast a foreboding pall.

"Why the crime watch, Lennard?" she asks out of concern.

"All the developments have one. Don't worry, you're perfectly safe here," Lennard answers reassuringly.

The Smile-A-Ride Shuttle passes by. A disgruntled white-haired man in a black t-shirt stares out of the window. Just then a bolt of lightning strikes, followed by rolling thunder.

20

Smile-A-Ride No More

Kim removes the shuttle schedule from the basket and calls to make a reservation. The following day, she enters the Smile-A-Ride Shuttle. Phil Capshaw, the driver, a kind but sweaty man with big round glasses is courteous and efficient. He welcomes Kim and asks if she needs his help. She assures him she's fine. To her surprise, Pat is already nestled in, a white beret in her lap, so she sits next to her.

Un-filtered Pat gets right to the point. "I don't mean to be nosy, now. But what happened to your leg?"

"Takayasu's Arteritis. It's a rare..." Before Kim can finish, Pat cuts her off.

"Everyone has Arthritis and those do-nothing doctors just take your money. 'Can't trust any one of them. Ugh!'"

There is no sense going on. It's evident she isn't interested. Not many people are. It is a rare disease. Very few people know what it is including those in the medical field. Except for the cane, there is no outside indication of disease.

As Kim's doctor noted before she left New York, "It hasn't beaten you up too badly yet. Stay away from steroids."

Kim takes his advice to heart.

The shuttle stops at the local supermarket.

"Your stop, Miss Wilson," Phil proclaims.

Pat springs from her seat, plops her white beret on her head, angles it to the side and in her singsong way declares, "Tonight it's

French food. I need eggs for the quiche. Au Revoir."

With her signature royal wave, she skips down the steps of the shuttle and with a bit of a hop exits it completely. Kim admires her energy. She settles back into a corner of the seat, removes her writer's magazine from her bag and begins to read.

Phil announces into his radio microphone, "Dispatch. This is 405. Minus Wilson, plus Gellis."

Kim peers out of the window. All she can see is the back of a large man with bushy white hair, cigarette in one hand reach over to Pat and try to hug her with the other. The door is open.

She hears him say, "Hi, Pattie. Where you been hiding?"

Pat squirms away. She looks frightened or is she angry? "Don't you touch me!"

The man holds on to her wrist. She pulls free, recoils and scoots away. The man chuckles and enters the shuttle with his lit cigarette. Kim buries her face in her writer's magazine.

Phil orders, "No smoking, Mr. Gellis."

"Sure, sure."

He takes a long sensuous drag on his cigarette and flips it through the open door.

Kim feels his eyes on her. She looks up at him. He pulls up his collar and wolf-whistles.

"Sit down and buckle up, Mr. Gellis," Phil suggests strongly.

Kim has a feeling of dread. She tries to focus on her magazine.

Although the shuttle is empty Mr. Gellis saunters over to where she is seated and sits close to her - too close. She feels his stale breath on her neck. Is he sniffing her? He is like an animal in heat. She squirms. Phil pulls out of the parking lot. She's had enough! She gathers her bag and her magazine, unlocks the seat belt and hobbles across the aisle.

"I can't continue if you are not in your seat and buckled up, miss," Phil notes.

"I'm sorry," She quickly buckles in.

Harry Gellis laughs, leans towards her and says, "Hubba, hubba. Me Harry, who you?"

"My name is Kim," she meekly divulges and pretends to read her magazine. She doesn't want to make him angry.

"Pretty name for a pretty lady, like Kim Novack, the actress. Where you off to?"

She looks at Phil. He's keeping an eye on them. She feels safe.

"Doctor's appointment."

"Ha!" Harry chortles. "I took medicine eight years in college and I still don't feel good."

She feels empowered now. "Are you the on-board entertainment?" The response shocks her.

"For you, doll-face, three shows a night."

Then Harry leans over and grabs her magazine out of her hands. She reaches for it. He teases her with it.

"Give me my magazine, please," she demands.

Harry ignores her request. "A writer? I got great stories. You can write them for me."

Angry now, she pulls the magazine away from him and declares, "I'm not looking for work."

To Phil, she begs, "Driver, how long to my destination?"

"Sit back, miss, we have a way to go."

"But my stories are better than the movies. Why don't you give me your card? I'll call you!" Harry continues.

"I don't have a card."

Kim thought the conversation was over and went back to reading her magazine, now folded and bent from the tug of war. Harry pulls out a deck of cards from his pocket. He shuffles them, fans them out and sticks them in front of her face.

Annoyed, she rolls up her magazine and places it on her seat.

"Pick one," Harry says joyfully.

He is like a child, an annoying child who demands attention – he wants to play. Anything to keep him at arm's length, she reluctantly chooses one.

"King of Hearts," she announces.

Harry turns the deck over. All the cards are kings of hearts with his address and phone number on them.

"My calling card. Keep it," he beams.

"No, thank you."

She leans forward and questions Phil again, "Driver, how much farther?"

Phil checks the mirror and responds, "We're almost there."

She seems relieved and settles back into her seat.

Harry leans over and murmurs quietly, "My wife died a few months ago and I miss her. I just wanted to talk to someone. 'Sorry I bothered you."

With his sudden change in behavior, Kim has the feeling he is overacting to elicit sympathy and make her feel guilty. He is successful. She succumbs to his act and for a moment thinks perhaps he is just a lonely old man looking for conversation.

"I am sorry to hear that," she utters.

"Yeah," he says sadly, "no one to talk to. Everyone around here is dead, just nobody told them yet."

"Perhaps, you could move somewhere else," she suggests.

"No! I can't. I've got this big job. Hundreds of people under me," Harry innocently blurts out.

Intrigued, Kim inquires, "Oh? What do you do?"

Harry begins to laugh. "I cut grass over at the cemetery."

"I'm glad you are having such a good time at my expense," she rebukes.

Harry turns on the charm. He flutters his eyelashes at her.

"Oh, c'mon. Don't be mad," he murmurs.

"I'll make it up to you. How 'bout I buy you lunch tomorrow?"

Incredulous, she states emphatically, "No thank you. I am a happily married woman."

"Who cares?" he quips.

"I do!"

The shuttle stops in front of a medical building.

Phil announces, "Your stop, Mrs. Wolf."

She is sorry he mentions her name. As she leaves her seat as quickly as possible and limps off the shuttle, she hears Phil talk to the dispatcher.

"Dispatch, this is 405, minus Wolf." To her dismay, he repeats her name.

Harry calls after her, "Hey, honey, just because there's snow on the roof, don't mean there's no fire in the furnace." He pauses then adds, "See ya' soon Mrs. Kim Wolf."

Ugh! What a horrible old man. He makes her skin crawl. She can't wait to get to her new doctor and home to Brad's strong and comforting arms.

21

Kim Meets Dr. Craig

It is the first time Kim is meeting her new internist who offers to be the gatekeeper for her health. She is building a new team of doctors which includes the internist, a rheumatologist, a neurologist and a cardiologist who will work together and share information. Other specialists will be added as needed. She is excited and frightened but has a residual negative memory from her encounter with Harry Gellis.

The office is spacious, clean and light. Classical music wafts through the waiting room. There is a beverage station offering coffee, tea, soup and hot chocolate near the entrance and a tray of cookies on a table nearby. A small refrigerator holds juice and bottles of water. There is a table filled with interesting current magazines. She is impressed and relaxes a bit.

Kim makes her way to the receptionists' window, introduces herself, checks in and is given what seems to be an endless amount of paperwork to complete. She takes a seat near the receptionists' station; there is no time for coffee or magazines, so she focuses on the paperwork.

The receptionists are engrossed in a discussion about their respective dating situations. From their conversation, Kim deduces that Deedee, no more than eighteen, an overweight, sexless know-it-all and Sally about twenty-five, an up-tight, repressed know-it-all, both have much to learn about life.

Upon completion of the all the forms, she heads back to the

reception area. With the standard clip board, completed paperwork attached, her bag and her cane, she trips but does not fall.

Sally slides the window open.

"Are you alright, Mrs. Wolf?" she inquires.

"I'm fine," she responds.

Kim hands Sally the paperwork and Sally includes it in a prepared file.

Kim continues. "'Just a bit anxious meeting my new doctor and on the shuttle on the way over here, an annoying elderly man tried to pick me up."

As soon as she says that she knows it is a mistake, but she is still upset. The two girls stifle giggles.

"Of course," Sally says sarcastically, "the doctor will see you right away. Room number one."

She buzzes Kim in. As Kim heads toward the examination room, Sally slides the glass closed and bursts into laughter.

Deedee adds in between giggles, "Who would flirt with a cripple?" Kim hears them.

Now, humiliated on top of feeling anxious, Kim tries to settle into the examining room, a step above the reception room in comfort. The walls are painted in a pleasing cool bluish gray color. A window frames a view of the mountains. Educational booklets are neatly housed in a wall organizer. There is a mini serenity garden on the counter. Within minutes, the doctor arrives, files in hand. He is young, about thirty-five, fit, blond, blue-eyed, pleasant and excited.

He extends his hand and says in a friendly manner, "Hello, I'm Dr. Craig."

He takes a moment to examine her with his eyes as he holds her hand. "I spoke to everyone on your medical team. Statistically, Takayasu's Arteritis has a high mortality rate. They're amazed at your recovery."

Kim takes a moment and examines him with her eyes. He exudes trust and sincerity.

She relaxes and replies, "I couldn't have done it without them."

As he tests her pulses she inquires "Am I your first Takayasu's patient?"

"Yes," He responds and without hesitation, adds, "I think we'll do just fine. I have the latest research."

Kim smiles while Dr. Craig tests her pulses.

"Why are you smiling?" Dr. Craig inquires.

"Just before we left New York, I had a flare up and was in the rheumatologist's office. Before I saw the doctor, a new young doctor was directed to test my pulses. He couldn't find any and bolted from the room in a panic."

"What happened?"

"I think he joined the priesthood."

Dr. Craig is amused. (Takayasu's is known as the "pulseless disease", because inflammation of blood vessels (vasculitis) can lead to absent or reduced pulses in the arms or legs).

"Tell me. What bothers you the most?"

The mood changes.

"The pain cycles are brutal, crippling. physically, mentally and emotionally. I can't function at all. I get so frustrated."

Dr. Craig listens intently; Kim sees compassion in his eyes. She calms down a little.

He continues his examination.

The subject changes.

"Tell me where you are from." He gently urges.

"I was born and raised in Brooklyn," she responds with a bit of hometown pride.

"Ah, famous Brooklyn, I'd like to visit there some day. Tell me, what is Hollywood's fascination with Brooklyn?" Dr. Craig inquires. He is deliberately distracting her.

"I've often wondered why so many films feature Brooklyn." As Kim speaks, he places a blood pressure cuff on her arm. She waits until he is done and records her blood pressure, Kim continues, "it was a good place in which to grow up."

"Mmmm." He is focused on her pressure. "It's a bit high."

Kim stays silent while he flips through her file and she wonders why he seems worried.

She quickly figures it out. "On the way over here, an elderly man was a bit aggressive."

He cuts her off and places a thermometer in her mouth.

"A calm emotional state is crucial to your ability to function," he lectures.

Then he makes notes in the folder. Kim remains silent and takes deep breaths. She is still upset by her encounter with Harry Gellis.

When Dr. Craig is through, he takes her hand and says, "We'll start your tests next week. Don't worry – we'll do fine. Remember, I want you to avoid stress as much as possible, try to exercise at least 30 minutes a day and drink plenty of water. When you venture outside, wear sunblock, sunglasses and carry water with you. You'd be amazed how quickly one becomes dehydrated in the desert heat."

Kim arrives home to find Brad frantically unpacking a teapot. They embrace.

Apologetically Brad laments, "I unpacked as much as I could, I missed you."

Kim kisses him. "I missed you, too."

She looks around and adds, "You did fine."

"How did it go with the new doctor?" Brad asks.

"I like him. He has all my records, is up-to-date on Takayasu's research and I'm back in a week for tests," Kim replies, "I'll be fine."

Kim removes her shoes and relaxes. The house is shaping up. Brad is doing a masterful job of organizing closets and drawers. She is pleased with Dr. Craig and happy with the move. She is eager to focus on Brad's burgeoning business. Brad is excited about going into his own business and is busy gathering clients.

The move to Arizona has been difficult for Brad. He desperately misses Manhattan but realizes the quality of life has changed and they (she) needs a different environment.

Kim recalls sharing with Brad what happened one morning shortly before they moved, Kim started to use a cane while she was still working. As she approached the building where she worked, a rude young man with a briefcase pushed her out of his way and slammed his briefcase into her leg so he could run in front of her to go through the revolving door. She recovered her balance, went in behind him and yanked the door to a stop. The young man was furious and frantically pointed to his watch. When she released the door, he screamed at her, "I have a meeting to go to!" She bravely replied, "If you were that important, they'd wait the ten seconds it took you to push me out of your way and smash your briefcase against my leg. Do you feel like a real man now?" With a huff, he made his way through the crowd and disappeared. He didn't care that he hurt her. She was shaken, bruised and in pain. Kim wasn't used to any sort of confrontation, but anger gave her a courage she hadn't experienced before. In less than a year, she was forced to resign, unable to continue to work full time.

She saw her team of doctors on an ongoing basis as they desperately tried to control her blood pressure, the pain cycles and rampant inflammation throughout her body. She was outside of the hospital one day, thinking about the story her rheumatologist just told her.

"I had a patient who wanted desperately to visit Italy but was afraid he'd get sick on the trip. Year after year he promised to go. He would discuss it with me, and I would encourage him to make the arrangements. Every year he found some excuse and kept putting it off basically out of fear. And then he died, never fulfilling his dream of seeing Italy."

"Why are you telling me this?" Kim asked.

"There is no known cure at this time and we're not coming up with the answers you need to be comfortable. I want you to focus on setting goals, long range goals. My advice to you is to not let any of your dreams die. Be smart, be strong, be brave. It's not going to get any easier."

Kim wanted to share that story with Brad. She entered a phone booth to report on the doctor's visit and share her new found enthusiasm. She placed her cane next to her leaning on the shelf of the telephone booth and called Brad. As the phone rang, two teenage boys came by, grabbed the cane from under her, ran into the nearest alley and tossed it to the end. She eventually retrieved it, scratched and dented but intact. That incident left a jagged cut in her confidence level.

Manhattan was no longer the city she adored. She was experiencing a cruelty, an anger she had never known, and her impairment was getting her into trouble; it was time to move on. As her dentist said, "New York is losing its sense of humor."

22

Settling In

Kim and Brad cuddle on the couch. Brad is excited and pleased that Kim likes Dr. Craig.

"Now, tell me about the antique center," she prods.

"I'll show you. The car is scrubbed, gassed and ready. Let's go for a ride!"

After an early romantic dinner at a luxury resort hotel, they take a gondola ride. Kim is fascinated that she is being serenaded by a gondolier in English and Italian as he steers them across the seven-acre lake in the middle of the desert. It is heavenly. She and Brad embrace, listen to the music and admire the beauty of the moonlight and its reflection on the water.

"I love how you love me. I feel so alive," Kim settles into Brad's arms and coos.

"Let's keep it that way," he says with tears in his eyes.

"I promise to stay around a long while," she assures him, and they hug tight.

She isn't going to let anything spoil her precious moments with Brad.

Afterward, they go for a ride to the antique center where Brad is about to launch his dream of owning his own antique business. He shows her around and scopes out his booth. Kim takes measurements and they plan how they will exhibit the inventory.

The evening is young; they stop for fresh flowers for the dining room table and agree to a hot game of Scrabble. When they arrive home, they set up their Scrabble game, listen to classical music, brew a pot of tea and settle in for a pleasant evening.

Brad challenges, "I'm gonna beat you this time."

Kim confidently teases, "That'll be a first. Good luck!"

Kim starts limping towards the table and loses her balance. Brad catches her, holds her tight and gently leads her into a dance. They laugh past the sadness and worry and focus on the game. She creates her first word, counts the letters and records her score.

Brad stares at her and inquires, "Have you told me everything the doctor said?"

"Yes. Why do you ask?"

"You seem preoccupied. I was hoping there were no more surprises," Brad says concerned.

"You know everything there is to know. It's just that on the way over there an obnoxious elderly man asked me for my number."

Brad smiles, plays a word and remarks, "He has good taste. You should be flattered. Add twelve to my score please."

She records the score and answers, "Well I'm not! It was like he has sex once a year and today was his day. Brrr."

They both laugh at that and Brad asks, "Are you serious?"

In between giggles, she mimics Harry and recalls, "He gave one of those wolf whistles and said hubba hubba."

Brad plays a word and questions, "How old would you say he is?" Kim records the score, makes a word and says, "Probably in his late seventies. He was like a sit-down comic with fetid breath and stale jokes."

As she talks more about Harry Gellis, she becomes less afraid. They continue playing and chatting.

"Maybe we should invite him over. Does he do impressions?"

"Nope, just stupid card tricks."

"He sounds harmless. Maybe he is just a lonely old guy trying too hard to be friendly," Brad insists.

Kim muses that over for a moment and continues playing.

She adds, "He did say his wife died recently. Maybe I am overreacting. You missed this.

Z A X and I am out!"

"Z A X? What's a Z A X?" Brad is taken by surprise.

"It's a tool used by roofers to punch nail holes in roofing slate."

"How do you know these things?"

"I saw it on the Internet. You are going to love it if I could ever get you to focus."

Sadly, Brad mumbles, "'Sorry, honey. You will have to forgive me. I am overwhelmed. I'm worried about this weekend. Maybe starting a new business now isn't so smart."

"Why wait?" she asks.

Brad strokes her hair tied in a bun on top of her head and insists she wear it long. He removes the pins holding it in place and her hair cascades down her back. They hug tight.

"Hubba, hubba!" Brad innocently says and then like a flash of lightening, she remembers something disturbing. An alarm bell in her gut goes off. She shudders. Is Harry Gellis the man on the tourist trolley the day she went to the volunteer office? She's confused, agitated.

Her mind starts to race. Didn't he throw his wife's ashes out the window? Does he live here? How does he know Pat? Who was that young man with him? What did they talk about? She desperately tries to remember their conversation.

Brad whispers, "The tighter you hold me, the freer I feel. You are right. Wait for what?"

Deep breaths. Stay calm. Dr. Craig's words resonate in her head. "A calm emotional state is crucial to your ability to function." Her energy and focus as always returns to Brad and she successfully pushes Harry Gellis and the scene with The Suit out of her thoughts as Brad and she kiss with passionate exploration. Brad carries her into the bedroom.

He places her gently on the bed next to a wrapped present. Like a child on Christmas morning, she swiftly unwraps the gift. It is a beautiful soft pink two-piece negligee. She can't wait to put it on even though she knows it will come off quickly.

23

Boys Night Out

We're at Sean's trailer home, me, Randi and Phil. It's small but impressive. Not only did Sean construct the trailer and install the electrical and plumbing, he built the furniture in it. All of which were made from the ribs of dead Saguaro cacti, with table tops made from slabs of red rock discarded in the desert. There are military medals, pins, emblems and patches on the walls, military magazines on the table alongside guns, knives and swords.

Sean pops open a half of a dozen beers, throws bags of chips on the couch and exclaims, "Divorce ain't so bad."

"Yeah, right," I say speaking from experience.

"Still cryin' in your beer?" prompts Randi as he snaps a new piece of chewing gum in his mouth.

"Nah, I got Betsy here to keep me company, right?" Sean picks up a shotgun, a heavy duty high gauge weapon and kisses it.

"Not the same, man." Phil is disturbed and paces around the small living room, drenched in sweat and wiping his glasses repeatedly.

"She's just like a woman. You gotta hold her good and tight or like my ex, she'll knock you on your butt." Sean poses with Betsy the shotgun and kisses it again.

"You could wipe out a small village with that!" Randi adds

"Yeah, like we need our villages to raise our kids. Right? Friggin' politicians. Hear what I'm sayin' dude?" Sean exclaims.

"Here we go again," Phil acknowledges as he continues to pace back and forth. Something must be troubling him. He's not eating.

"You're laughin' now Phil. The new millennium is coming. There's gonna be a revolution."

With a disgusted, angry face, Sean continues, "We gotta be ready!"

"Phil could have used that on the shuttle today." Randi deduces as an afterthought.

"Why? What happened?" I am intrigued.

"You know Harry Gellis, the pain in the ass on Quaking Aspen?" Phil paces faster as he recalls the event.

"'Don't know him." I said. I am unfamiliar with the residents and assume they are all elderly retirees. I quickly lose interest in the conversation and browse through a gun collector's magazine.

"You mean the hairy guy who talks too loud and stares a lot? Dude, what about him?" Sean insists.

"He tried to strangle me!" Phil continued his pacing and massages his neck.

"Why?" Sean asks incredulously.

"He hit on Mrs. Wolf, the new woman."

"The crippled lady?" Sean says,

"Wolf? Kim? "I know that name.

"Yeah, Kim Wolf. Why? You know her?" Randy prompts me.

"She's one of my volunteers at the station. Was she hurt?" I inquire.

Phil added, "Nah. I mean he was all over her. I was going to step in, but she handled it okay."

"Yeah she got off the shuttle," Randi adds and laughs.

"Did you file a report with the police?" I ask.

"No one got hurt and I gotta keep this in-house." Randi is all business.

"How come?" Sean asks.

"Job security. We've got houses to sell. The last thing we need is to have people know we have jerks like that living at Pima Vista." He adds another piece of gum to his rotating jaw.

"He's just a harmless old guy with a big mouth. We could put a scare into him – for the fun of it. You hear me?" Sean aims the shotgun at an invisible target. "Pow, pow!"

"Don't do anything stupid, Sean." Randi seems concerned.

"Well, we gotta do something! Let me tell you what he did to me!" Phil cries.

"Let's not rehash this thing. I made the report." Randi is annoyed.

"No! Guys you gotta hear this." Phil begs for attention.

Phil is animated now pacing up and down in the small trailer. He actually is putting on a little play for us as he recalls the incident, playing both himself and Harry Gellis.

"So, I pulled out of the parking area where I left off Mrs. Wolf."

He mimics Harry Gellis by wildly gesturing and changing his voice as he plays each part.

"Hey, Phil. Where'd you pick up Wolf?"

"No talking to the driver while the shuttle is in motion," I shot back.

"What's the big deal? Where does she live?"

"We don't give out resident information. Besides, you shouldn't be robbing the cradle," I said which I thought was funny.

Then I stopped at a red light. Apparently, Harry didn't think it was funny because he bolted from his seat, grabbed me by the collar and yanked me backwards. My glasses flew off my face. I was shocked and a little bit scared. The guy's an animal and strong as an ox!"

Phil has everyone's attention. We're all laughing and enjoying the show. I'm not so sure Phil is but he continues.

"It's a simple question four-eyes. Where does she live?" Harry screamed at me.

"The light turns green. Drivers are honking me and I'm struggling with Harry. The guy is trying to strangle me! The honking continues. I know I'm turning red. I'm afraid I'm gonna pass out. He's got me pinned to the seat."

"So, then what happened?" Sean is into the story chin resting on Betsy.

Randy chews away, spits out his old gum and tosses a new piece in his mouth and I'm watching the whole scene wondering where it's all going.

Phil continues. "All of a sudden Harry decides to take a seat and he's belly laughing. I think he's crazy. I fumble for my glasses, park the van and shout over the microphone 'Dispatch, dispatch! This is 405. Send help! I'm at the Mescal Medical Center. Hurry!' Harry just sat there laughing. I drove back to the parking lot, put on the hazard lights and bolted from the shuttle. Harry placed his arms behind his head, leaned back, put his big feet on the seat across from him and watched out the window while I waited for Randi."

Phil was finished. A moment of silence then we all clapped simultaneously. Phil looks baffled for a brief time then bows.

"I'm there within minutes," Randi announces. "I quickly approach Phil. He is roughed up and angry."

"Well do you blame me for being angry?" Phil whined. "I get to work in a good mood thinking I'll have an easy day and all hell breaks loose." He grabs his neck and massages it. He advances his story. "So, I'm standing in the parking lot telling Randi what happened, and the ape is mocking me through the window."

I feel badly for Phil. Sean can hardly catch his breath he is laughing so hard.

Randi takes over. "Harry is mimicking a stressed-out Phil while Phil is waving his arms telling me what happened on the shuttle. I listen intently arms folded but keeping an eye on Harry just in case there are any sudden moves."

"I don't need this crap, man!" Phil's yelling at me.

Focused on my Glock he suggests, "Maybe *I* should carry a gun." That got a big laugh.

"Take my truck back to the office and fill out a report," I order. "Phil and I exchange keys and Phil speeds away in my truck."

Phil composed now sits on the arm of the couch and munches on chips. As Randi describes the aftermath of the attack, Phil nods his head in agreement.

Randi goes on with the drama. "I took a moment sized up the situation and entered the shuttle. Harry stood up immediately and eyed my Glock. "Have a piece of gum, Mr. Gellis," I offered."

"Nah." He tried to push my hand away. I knew what I was dealing with. I chewed a new piece of gum and waited.

It was interesting. We are both large men; I'm muscular fit and strong. Harry is large and strong and about 25 years older than me. We stood toe to toe eye to eye, neither of us afraid of verbal confrontation nor physical battle. Clearly, we both have experience, mine is as a patriot. I'm not sure what his is. I think he's a bunch of hot air; he blinked first."

"You know what's wrong with Phil?" Harry asks.

"Tell me," I respond coolly.

"No respect! In my neighborhood, if he treated anyone the way he treated me, they'd find his ass bouncing off the waves in Coney Island," Harry threatens.

"Well, Mr. Gellis, why don't you tell me exactly what happened," I suggest.

Randi can't resist. He, too impersonates Harry Gellis' posture and we're all laughing. Randi spreads out his hands like Harry and speaks in a weird voice with a bad New York accent. "It's real simple, see? I got up to ask him a question and lost my balance."

In military stance I held my ground. "Phil says you choked him and knocked his glasses off his face."

With a clumsy attempt at charm, Harry declares, "Nah. I fell against him and had to grab him so's to break my fall. Really, it was an accident."

"I have to report this incident, Mr. Gellis," I warn him.

"Who cares? 'Just get me to the bank before it closes."

"Sit down and buckle up, Mr. Gellis," I demand. "He just glares at me."

"I don't take orders from nobody." "He folds his arms like a petulant teen.

I place my hand casually on my Glock and caution him," "Can't have another accident Mr. Gellis."

"Harry receives my message. I wink at him and hold out a piece of gum."

"Have a piece of gum." "Begrudgingly, he yanks the gum out of my hand and buckles in. The power had shifted. I drive out of the parking lot and onto the street, just me and Harry on the way to the bank."

The story is over. We all simultaneously clap and head out to the Mustang Bar a small, noisy western bar.

24

Who's Lydia and What happened to Her?

It's the day after the Smile-A-Ride incident. Lennard and Sean arrive at the Wolf's house. Kim is busy unpacking dishes. Lennard holds a brown paper bag and directs Sean to spray for insects.

"You'll have to spray often to get rid of the crickets," Lennard advises.

"They seem harmless enough," she naively observes.

''Sorry, ma'am. Crickets attract scorpions, scorpions attract rattlesnakes." Lennard gently educates her.

"I like to shoot those suckers and blow their heads off!" Sean interjects as he continues spraying throughout the house.

"Why don't you finish up in the other rooms?" Lennard suggests to Sean.

"Sure, boosss!"

The way Sean pronounced boss, the friction between Lennard and Sean is obvious to Kim.

"Right between the eyes. Splat!" Sean is laughing now.

Lennard represses his anger.

"Sorry about Sean. We didn't mean to scare you," Lennard apologizes.

"You didn't. I thought roaches, water bugs and rats were rough," she assures him.

"You had rats?" Lennard inquires.

"No. Roaches and water bugs rented space in my apartment building. The rats were guests of the city.

78

"I don't understand," Sean replies.

"When I refer to the City, I mean Manhattan which is a small island approximately twenty three square miles; around thirteen miles in length and under two and one half miles wide. Yet millions of people, live and work on it and travel to and from there on a daily basis, often eating from street food vendors. Rats are inevitable given the amount of people concentrated in such a small space surrounded by a busy waterway."

"Wow!" Was all Lennard could say.

Kim continues, "New York City consists of five boroughs; Manhattan, Brooklyn, Queens, The Bronx and Staten Island. Collectively, the population of over 8 million people occupy over 300 plus square miles. Keep in mind that New York City is just a small section of New York State."

"How does it accommodate so many people?" Lennard inquires.

Kim looks up and points. "Skyscrapers. They build up." She adds thoughtfully, "Yes, living and working in New York City was exhilarating and exhausting."

Just then her computer beeps in the den.

"What's that?" Lennard asks.

Kim escorts Lennard to the den.

"My computer; automatic Internet reconnect."

"Pretty cool. I meant to ask Mr. Wolf about surge protectors." Lennard makes a note.

Sean follows them around mumbling, "Pow, pow! Right between the eyes, ha ha ha."

Lennard ignores him. Kim interprets it as a threat towards Lennard.

"We've got surge guard, line protection and back-up power."

"You're pretty hi-tech," Lennard acknowledges with admiration.

He hands her the brown paper bag.

"By the way, this is for you and Mr. Wolf - a little house-warming gift."

Like an excited child on her birthday, Kim eagerly unwraps the gift. She is like that with gifts and sweets, particularly ice-cream, remnants of her happy childhood.

Kim holds up a beautiful colorful round woven disc covered in leather. She admires the multicolored beads and feathers attached.

"Ooh, pretty. What is this?" she inquires.

Lennard just smiles. "It's a dream catcher. You hang it on your bed. It catches the bad dreams and allows the good ones through."

"It looks like a spider web," she observes.

"Yes, that is exactly what it represents. A protective web used to shield sleeping children. I'm told it was started by the Ojibwe people; you may know them as Chippewa. The Lakotas have their tradition as well. Most Native Americans use them," Lennard adds.

"What a wonderful tradition and such a thoughtful thing to do. Thank you so much." She is deeply touched.

In the reflection of the window, Kim notices Sean mimicking her. He is a slimy little turd bent on stealing the slightest bit of happiness out of the room. She snaps around to catch him. He turns his back on her.

He could have been embarrassed.

"I'm done," he mumbles.

Kim believes Lennard saw the same thing she did, but always the gentleman, just calmly nods and instructs Sean.

"Meet me back at the office, please."

As Sean exits, mumbling incoherently, Pat swoops in wearing a wide brimmed straw hat, beige capri pants and a wildly colorful short sleeve shirt.

"My, my Lennard. You are becoming a regular here," she slyly suggests.

"When duty calls, Miss Wilson."

Ignoring Lennard, Pat prattles on, but she isn't really smiling. She's fishing. Did Kim note a look of fear?

"Well, Kim, tell us about your encounter with Gellis the menace."

"He practically sat in my lap. Who is he?" she replies with slight annoyance.

Lennard is quick to respond.

"'Just an old guy who tells corny jokes and thinks he's a lady's man. He's harmless."

Pat was quick to retort.

"My friend Lydia didn't think so and got it all wrong. That's why I joined Crime Watch!"

She was hiding something. Kim wants to know more but before she could speak, Lennard quickly states.

"Really? I wouldn't be spreading rumors, Miss Wilson."

Pat is angry now. She reacts quickly.

"It's no rumor."

They have Kim's attention. She wants more information.

"Who is Lydia and what happened to her?" she inquires.

Pat appears to be annoyed, embarrassed, a bit mixed-up and quickly morphs into her public persona.

"Ohhh. I can't go over it right now. Lennard, you tell her. Gotta trot. I'm cooking Spanish tonight; I have to separate the gravel from the beans. Adios!"

With her signature wave, Pat vanishes like a puff of smoke.

Kim faces Lennard. "Tell me about Harry Gellis."

She's unable to read him, but he is uncomfortable speaking about Harry Gellis.

"Lydia claimed that someone broke into her house and molested her. It was reported to the police. First, she accused Mr. Gellis of the crime, then promptly changed her story and moved away after meeting with his business manager. That's all I know."

"Harry Gellis has a business manager? Do you think there is anything to it?" Kim probes.

"Frankly, I think it was all in her head. Many of the older ladies who live here alone often call us with unfounded reports of prowlers, lurking strangers, etc. I understand. They're scared, lonely and need attention." He checks his watch and adds, "I'd better go now, too."

"Of course. Thank you. Have a good day," Kim says.

They say their good-byes. Kim escorts Lennard out and locks the door thinking to herself.

"Maybe Crime Watch isn't such a bad idea."

25
Pat's Dilemma

The next morning, Pat and Kim go together to the swimming pool for the aquasize class. Kim's doctors encouraged her to exercise in water. The pool is perfect, and Kim is thrilled to attend her first session. But first she has business to attend.

Neither food nor drink is allowed in the pool area but there is a section nearby that accommodates vending machines and a snack bar. Just outside of that area is a bulletin board with announcements of club meetings, upcoming events and a space for residents to tack on their business cards. Kim posts the announcement of the opening of the new antique center and Brad's newly printed business card. She is so proud.

The Olympic sized pool is beautifully kept, surrounded by lush desert plants, riverbed rock and boulders. The pool area is vast with cabanas, several seating arrangements, umbrellas and a fire pit lit during evening hours. Music is played through an elaborate sound system. The pool is large enough that classes could be conducted at one end and residents could swim freely at the opposite end without disturbance. The setting is stunning with a backdrop of swaying palm trees against the everchanging pastel shaded skies. It is like being on vacation.

The class is given by the activities' director, Mitzi Benson. Mitzi, late fifties is curvy, perky, single and physically fit. She has shoulder length curly brunette hair, and big bright blue eyes. An attractive woman, she exudes a positive energy. As the Activities Director, she is quite popular, visible and busy. Kim marvels at her ability to balance all the demands made of her by staff and residents.

Pat insists on introducing Kim to Mitzi. True to form, Pat introduces them and rambles on about Kim being from Manhattan which is totally unnecessary and time consuming given that they are about to start a class. Mitzi is gracious and welcomes Kim warmly. Mitzi suggests Kim stay close to her during the class, so she could follow her instructions easily and she could work with her if needed.

The class begins on time. There are about a dozen people of varied ages in the class. Kim is introduced to everyone and accepted cordially. Pat stays by Kim's side and takes her welfare as her personal responsibility. It is a kind thing to do.

Pat is the only one wearing a swim cap, bright yellow with large plastic pink and green flowers on the top. Mitzi leads the class through several exercises and Kim is feeling comfortable and proud that she is able to keep up. Mitzi calls instructions, "Now jog in place, 1,-2, 1,-2, 1,-2. Now hands in the water and scull, push pull, push pull."

For Kim it is exhausting but she's getting into the rhythm of the exercises.

Pat leans over and whispers, "Guess who called me asking for your number."

"I have no idea," Kim responds while struggling to keep up.

With an odd mixture of annoyance and sarcasm, Pat points to the far end of the pool and says, "Handsome Harry."

Kim is flabbergasted. There is Harry Gellis in a too tight bathing suit climbing to the high board. He jumps up and down on the board creating loud noises as the board rebounds against the fulcrum. She loses her place and stops exercising.

"Oh no," is all she can say.

Pat continues, "He called me last night. I imagine Harry, cigarette in one hand, telephone in the other slouched on his torn recliner next to a table covered with sleazy girlie magazines, over-flowing ashtrays and the remnants of a TV dinner."

"That's quite a description," Kim comments.

"I ought to know. I spent enough time over there to know his habits. I was right in the middle of cooking a new middle eastern dish. I had several pots on the stove, the television was on, the air conditioner was running at full blast and the ceiling fans whirled noisily. The phone must have rung ten times before I heard it. I almost tripped on the kitchen mat as I tried to lower the volume of the television, so I could hear him. You'll appreciate this. The conversation went something like,

Harry: "Hi, Pattie! It's handsome Harry."

Pat: "I'm not talking to you."

Harry: "C'mon Pattie. You're not still mad at me for tearing your panties, are you?"

Pat: "My name is Pat and yes, I am."

Harry: "Well I won't bother you anymore."

Pat: "Is this an apology?"

Harry: "Hell, no!"

Pat: "Then why are you calling me?"

Harry: "I want Kim Wolf's number."

Pat: "I don't have it and I wouldn't give it to you if I did!"

Harry: "Frigid witch. I'll fix you, too."

"He threatened you?" Kim uttered!

"Can you imagine?"

"Aren't you worried?"

"Of course not. He won't do anything; he's just a big tease, so I didn't take it seriously. I slammed the phone down, tripped over a wire and dropped a wooden spoon before I went back to my cooking. Sometimes, he makes me so mad. So, it's good I made him a little mad. Let him know how it feels."

"Are you and Harry an item?"

Mitzi notices Kim and Pat whispering. "Keep up, ladies."

Kim and Pat focus on the exercise routine.

Wistfully, Pat divulges, "I thought we had a good thing going, me and Harry. I can overlook his rough edges and teach him some manners maybe. He's quite handsome, don't you think?" Without waiting for an answer, Pat blathers on. "He's got some nice qualities and a good sense of humor, a bit cynical for me..." She seemed to wander off into space. Kim touches her lightly and whispers "Pat?" As if nothing happened, Pat continues, "I was hoping he'd consider moving in with me and we could take care of each other. Do you understand me?"

Kim is surprised to learn that Pat has warm feelings towards and such an intimate history with Harry. It is all a huge misunderstanding and Kim doesn't want Pat to be angry with her.

"I'm so sorry, Pat. I wish he would just leave me alone!" Kim pleads.

"So, do I. There aren't many single men here and those of us who are single don't appreciate young married women horning in on them and luring them away, do you understand?"

"Pat, of course I understand, I have no interest in Harry Gellis and would never 'horn in' as you put it in anyone else's relationship. You can have him!"

Kim is embarrassed and angry that Pat thinks she could ever be attracted to Harry

"Okay, maybe I am mistaken about you," Pat allows.

"One hundred percent! I am in love with Brad, always have been – always will be."

"Okay, I guess I believe you."

Mitzi continues her directions, while focused on Harry.

"Good, now tell me about Lydia and the crime watch," Kim probes.

"Lydia was mistaken about Harry. He doesn't need to sneak around and attack women. In fact, he can have any woman here if he wants them. That's why I joined Crime Watch. It must have been someone from the outside," Pat explains.

Mitzi stops the class and shouts, "The diving boards are closed during the aquasize class, Mr. Gellis."

Harry continues to bounce up and down on the board smiling and waving. The classmates are annoyed and growing impatient.

"Mr. Gellis, please!" Mitzi cries in desperation.

Harry cups his mouth and yells back, "Do you want me to stop?"

"Yes!" Mitzi replies.

"Isn't he a hoot?" Pat says admiringly.

Kim smiles weakly.

Apparently satisfied that Harry will comply, Mitzi is about to continue the class when Harry springs off the board in a cannonball dive and creates a huge splash which sends spray and waves through the exercise class. He surfaces and swims over to them.

"Oops, I slipped," Harry says as he winks.

"Not funny, Mr. Gellis," Mitzi declares.

"Whaddya goin' to do? Report me?"

He climbs out of the pool, flops down into a lounge chair and stares straight at Kim.

"That's exactly what I am going to do."

Mitzi returns her attention back to the class and shouts a new set of instructions. The students obey. Kim struggles to concentrate while Harry stares at her and she loses her place which amuses him.

"Stretch right 1,-2,-3,-4. Left 1,-2,-3,-4. Repeat!" Mitzi orders.

Pat leans over and sneers, "He seems hot on you."

"Pat, please," Kim begs. "Your friendship is far more important to me than Harry Gellis' fantasy about me. I'm simply not interested in him."

"We'll see," Pat threatens.

Mitzi ends the class. "That's it. Wonderful class everybody. Same time, next time."

They all applaud and exit the pool. Kim wraps herself in a towel, grabs her cane and attempts to keep up with Pat and the other ladies as they head towards the locker room. Harry jumps in front of Kim and Pat and does a poor imitation of a body building pose.

"It's a good thing you are wearing that towel, Mrs. Kim Wolf," Harry teases. "I wouldn't want to get too excited - I may bust a seam."

He looks down at his crotch, winks and nods.

"I suggest you take a cold shower Harry Gellis," Kim retorts sharply.

He moves out of their way and bows.

"Well excuuuse me," he attempts to be funny.

He turns to Pat.

"Hey, Pattie. What the hell are you wearing? You look like a Miss America reject," He cruelly says, a bit too loud.

Pat slithers up to him and seductively suggests, "Why don't you come over tonight? I'll make your favorite dish – spaghetti and meatballs with that new sauce you like."

"Nah. I'm still mad at you – you know why," Harry responds flirtatiously.

"Well then, why don't you take another jump in the pool and don't bother to come up." Pat is hurt but lingers as Mitzi dressed in shower clogs and a bright windbreaker over her swimsuit passes them quickly and approaches Harry.

She speaks up in an authoritative tone, "Mr. Gellis. I don't appreciate you disrupting my class."

"Mr. Gellis is it? Hey, I told you, I slipped," Harry mockingly answers.

"Next time, watch your step," Mitzi threatens. "There's always a next time. Say wonder woman, how about you and me take your car to Mexico for the weekend and straighten out that complaint you filed?" Harry suggests.

"Don't be ridiculous!"

"I'll have my business manager contact you and we'll work it out."

"Don't bother. You're not worth my time."

Mitzi turns her back and begins to walk away. Harry grabs her arm.

"A smooth paint job will take ten years off a woman's age, but you can't fool a flight of steps."

Mitzi removes Harry's hand from her arm.

"You've been eating too many fortune cookies. Good day, Mr. Gellis."

Mitzi and Pat walk together back towards the locker room. Pat laments, "He promised to take me to Mexico, too."

"Lezzie, dyke!" Harry snorts. I'll get even with you too, bitch!"

All the women hear him.

Harry imitates Mitzi's strut. He loiters by the locker rooms for a while and watches as Mitzi, Kim and Pat enter. He then wanders over to the vending machines and gleefully removes both the antique center opening announcement and Brad's business card. "Bingo!" He exclaims.

26

Locker Room Chatter

The locker room is a hub of information, gossip, conjecture and so-called fact espoused by interesting women. It is doubtful Kim can find three sources to check for each story. Opinion rules.

Harry Gellis is the focus of conversation, led by Mitzi. No surprise to Kim, she hears that Harry has made a lot of enemies in the development; particularly, with staff. He frequently disobeys the rules and creates problems for them. Simple rules like no smoking, curbing his garbage cans, no drinking by the pool, etc. Harry seems determined not only to ignore the rules, but to break them as often as possible.

Where the residents are concerned, he is rude to the men, has no friends and is not a member of any club or organization available as part of the amenities. He played in the billiard room once, accused the other resident of cheating and deliberately tore the felt on the pool table. It was repaired by his business manager, Mr. Grimm. Harry is banned from playing.

As far as the women are concerned, Harry fancies himself a desirable man and for his age, he is. Because of his size, physical power and fearlessness he exudes the promise of protection imbued with a bad-boy image which some women find attractive. He flirts with all the women, dated several of the single women and is rumored to have had a tryst with one of the married women. Pat insists he is misunderstood; she is willing to overlook his crude behavior and dismisses much of the negative comments from the women as jealousy.

Mitzi, Pat and Kim change out of their bathing suits, shower, dress and line up in front of the mirrors to do their hair and apply make-up.

Carla, a tall, ultra-thin, flat chested woman, known as the bookworm, drifts by them. She has small facial features, a button nose, thin lips, and short, thinning hair. Her bulging blue piercing eyes are anchored behind thick black framed glasses. She has her nose in a book even as she walks. She is known to recite interesting but totally useless information.

Pat grabs Carla's arm and stops her. "Meet my new neighbor, Kim!" Carla stares at Kim and examines her closely before she responds. To fill the dead air, Pat continues, "Carla is in charge of Book Club. We meet once a month – it's fun. You should sign up."

"Oh, yes, do. We're always looking for new members," Carla finally speaks.

"Thank you. I'll think about it, but my husband and I are quite busy setting up a new business," Kim responds.

Carla continues, "You're the new people. I saw your husband's card next to the flyer for the antique center opening. So, he is in the watch business," she states authoritatively. "Do you know when the first pilot's wristwatch was created?"

"Yes, I do." Kim rises to the challenge.

Pat pops up. "Tell us!" She addresses no one in particular.

Both Carla and Kim start to speak at the same time. In unison, they say, "In 1904…"

Kim stops and gives Carla the floor. She is sure Carla has more details than she.

Carla coolly continues. She enjoys an audience. The locker room becomes quiet.

"Picture this. Aviation is young. We've all seen photos of the original flying machines from the Wright Brothers on. Early pioneer aviators testing emerging aircraft such as monoplanes, biplanes and gyroplanes doing their best to rise higher and higher, stay in the air longer and longer and fly greater and greater distances; the French, the British and the Americans all competing to conquer the skies.

Imagine the skill and focus it took attempting to check their flying time against the speed of travel. All they have are pocket watches. With both eyes and hands on the controls, clumsily and dangerously, they have to remove the pocket watches from their flying suits to measure the time."

There was silence as they all imagined a lone flyer at the controls wearing heavy goggles, perhaps gloves, dressed in a flying suit with zippered or buttoned pockets, fussing to remove a watch with a hinged case which needs two hands to open.

"An aviator named Alberto Santos-Dumont solicited help from a French jeweler named Louis Cartier. Cartier took the challenge and developed the first pilot's wrist watch. Story over, ladies."

"But, Carla," Kim says, "do you know that the earliest wrist watches were created for ladies while men used pocket watches?"

"No! I didn't know that," Carla responds. "I'll check that out." She puts her head back into her book and goes to the end of the lockers to finish dressing. She looks like a walking x-ray.

Kim likes Carla and the way she builds up a story. She is eager to access her computer and read all she can about Cartier and his aviator watch. She is correct about Carla having more information than she. Kim had forgotten the aviator's name but remembered it was Louis Cartier who developed the pilot's wristwatch. Brad has two Cartier Pashas for sale, circa 1980s. Carla's story would be an added fun fact for a potential customer.

Back to the mirrors and make-up. "You're the garbage lady from New York, aren't you?" Mitzi inquires.

"I beg your pardon?" Kim states.

"Every time I walk my dog on recycle day, I check your recycle bin. You have the best garbage. I get great satisfaction at checking out your recyclables."

"I'm glad you approve."

"I do!"

Kim is not comfortable with people knowing so much about her personal habits and intends to do a better job of placing recyclables in plain sight.

As Carla walks past them again, Mitzi whispers, "She never showers."

"What?" Kim is shocked. She didn't sense an odor.

"'Just whore's baths. I've seen her," Mitzi confides.

"Maybe she doesn't like to shower in public. By the way, what's a whore's bath?"

Animated Mitzi pretends to wash under her arms and in between her legs.

"How do you know that?"

"Not all of us were assistants to the rich and famous in New York."

"I see. What did you do before you retired?"

"I was an exotic dancer and a stripper in Vegas. That's how I know about putting on shows and doing hair and makeup."

"And the whore's baths?"

"A girl's gotta eat."

"I'm sorry, Mitzi."

"Don't be. I have no regrets."

Kim dismisses the conversation and focuses on her new task to research the history of watches for Brad. Lost in thought, she drops the hair dryer and the brush. Pat and Mitzi to the rescue.

"Are you ok?" Pat asks, concerned.

"Maybe I overdid it a little. I'm in my dropping and tripping phase. I'll be alright. I just need to sit for a while," Kim relates.

"You poor thing," Pat says.

"Sit down, we'll help you," Mitzi suggests.

"I'm fine. It passes," she reassures Pat and Mitzi who are keeping close eyes on her.

May I do your hair?" Mitzi inquires.

"She's good," Pat announces. "She produces all our shows <u>and</u> does hair and make-up."

"Kim, we are always on the lookout for talented people. Do you sing and da…?" Pat gasps, Mitzi stops short, terribly embarrassed.

Kim ignores her faux pas.

"Neither. My strength is behind the scenes, writing, organizing, researching." No need to embarrass her any more than she embarrassed herself.

"Well then, perhaps we can get you to edit the script for our next show."

"Perhaps," she agrees.

"In the meanwhile, why don't you come to our seventies party Friday night? Wear your bell bottoms and, Pat, you can disco to dawn," Mitzi announces.

"Great, I still have my love beads."

Pat is giddy with excitement until Mitzi reminds her, "That was the sixties, dear."

"Silly, me. I get everything mixed up."

"An easy mistake," Kim verbalizes. For some reason, Kim wants to protect Pat. She knows she is getting on in years and alone. She just doesn't want her to think she's stealing Harry away from her.

"It's a good thing Mitzi plans everything," Pat adds. "I'd botch it all up."

Mitzi retains her strut.

"That's my life. Social director extraordinaire. I even open the pool every morning."

Kim regains her strength and balance and rises to leave. As she gathers her belongings, Mitzi inquires of Pat, "So, what did our resident lothario say to you?"

"Nothing I care to repeat."

Out of curiosity, Kim questions Mitzi.

"Mitzi, do you know Harry Gellis well?"

Mitzi hesitates, then offers.

"I know Harry Gellis a little, dislike him a lot. He's all grab and no feelings. I've had problems with him. He likes to play rough."

"If you took the time to get to know him better," replies Pat, "You'd see he's not a bad guy."

"I disagree. You know why he gets so mad?" Mitzi inquires.

"No," answers Pat

"Because he's all talk; he just can't get it up!"

"He doesn't have that problem with me, but he is in an awful hurry," brags Pat.

"You know what he told me?" Mitzi teasingly asks.

"No, tell me," Pat says eagerly.

"A long time ago, Harry confided in me that he is not looking for a long-term relationship and that once he had all the single women here, he would move. But that he had one more woman to conquer."

Pat mused that statement over and said, "You know who it must have been?"

They answer in unison, "Lydia!"

Kim let that settle in. Being single at their age cannot be easy. She is still baffled by the Lydia story and wants to know more.

Their conversation is amusing to her, talking so openly about their sexual escapades, but she is uneasy about Harry Gellis.

27

Ponytails in Paradise

Kim is concerned about the way she is feeling and focuses on strength to get home, work on the computer and prepare dinner, even though she knows Brad will take over if she is unable to cook. He is doing more than she could have hoped for and she is becoming weaker and weaker. She made a mental note to speak to Dr. Craig about her declining energy.

She rushes home eager to research watches on her computer. Wrist watches is sometimes spelled as one word, sometimes two, like the words post card and screen play. Early on, when one wanted to place ads on the Internet, there was a limit to the amount of characters one could use. Kim had been researching sites and placing ads for Brad and to be creative in her descriptions and to save precious space, she listed the word wristwatch as one word.

In the beginning of the Internet, there is oversight and one is expected to use proper grammar and spelling. It is Kim's understanding that initially the Internet is set up for universities to communicate. Once the opportunity for commerce arises, Kim explores it and plans to create a site for Brad to have a business presence on the Net. She begins with ads to buy and sell. She is making headway and communicating with other watch enthusiasts who are eager to exchange knowledge and/or do business. After dinner, she and Brad review the emails and Brad conducts his business.

To Kim's chagrin, she receives a notice that she is banned from using the Internet for her use of vulgar language. She is horrified, humiliated and worried not only that Brad's reputation will be damaged, but that all their work will be lost, and his dream of expanded business is in jeopardy.

She responds immediately to the email message and begs for clarity. It takes days to resolve. Eventually she is told that her use of the word wristwatch contains a vulgar word related to a woman's body part. Her first experience with algorithms. From then on, whenever she has any ads or correspondence related to wrist watches, she uses the two word method form.

More stress.

Later that evening as she sits on a stool and cleans the pots from dinner, she casually mentions to Brad that she wants to cut her hair short. Using her reacher to get a roll of paper towels, she is stunned by Brad's response.

"You can't!" he shouts.

She drops the reacher and the towels and almost falls off the stool.

Brad retrieves the reacher and the towels after making sure she is secure on the stool.

"That's exactly why I want to cut my hair. I can't handle it anymore. I dropped the hair dryer and my brush in the locker room today. I'm so clumsy now, it's embarrassing."

He softens.

"I understand but if you cut your hair it's like I'm losing you piece by piece!"

She relents. He is suffering. It breaks her heart.

"Okay, I won't. Relax," she assures him.

"Promise?" he challenges.

"Promise," she reassures him. "I hope you like ponytails."

"I do." Brad grins and changes the painful subject.

"So, how was your aqua-size class today?"

"Great, until that jerk disrupted it." She can't hide her disdain.

"The old guy? Did he bother you again?"

"No. He made some sophomoric remarks and insulted Pat."

"Ignore him. I'm sure he is harmless." Brad waves him away.

Changing the subject again, Brad asks for the fiftieth time, "Are we ready for the opening tomorrow?"

"All items have been researched, described in detail and priced appropriately. We have color coded tags and inventory lists. We will leave early, set up the case and be ready for the grand opening. Let's get some rest. Tomorrow is your big day."

"I'm excited and a bit scared of the opening."

"No need. We are as prepared as we can be. We will know if we have an audience for our merchandise soon enough. But whatever happens, just know that I am proud of all you have accomplished and together we will make it all work."

He takes big breaths and smiles at her.

He walks to the window. The sun is setting. He is calming down but a bit excited.

"Come look at this gorgeous sunset!" he exclaims.

He leads her off the stool and holds her as they gaze at the sky.

"Isn't this paradise?" As they snuggle, he plays with her hair.

28

Harry's Revenge, Mitzi Pays

It is dark outside. The pool area is locked. Harry, dressed in black from head to toe places a flashlight in his mouth and with a lock pick, opens the gate and creeps into the filter room. Once inside the filter room, Harry locates the control panel. Plastic containers filled with liquid chlorine line the shelves over a workbench scattered with tools.

He opens the filter control panel and removes the "Off" tripper from the timer. CREAK! He hears the pool gate open and close. He takes a large pipe wrench from the work table and hides behind the door.

Lennard enters the pool area, flashlight in hand. He inspects the property around the pool. Harry remains behind the door, ready to strike. Lennard opens the door, does not enter but scans the room with his flashlight, finds nothing of any concern, closes the door and exits the pool area.

Harry stands mute until he hears the noise of the pool gate open and close. When he is satisfied that he is alone, he puts the filter in backwash mode. He starts the pump and causes water in the pool to be pumped into the sewer. He then proceeds to open several containers of chlorine and tip them over. With a handkerchief to his mouth, he exits as fumes fill the room.

The next morning, Mitzi, the aquasize instructor, enters the pool area, focuses on the half empty pool and enters the filter room. She attempts to turn off the pumps. With eyes burning and overcome by the fumes, she stumbles toward the exit and collapses.

"Help me, somebody help me!" Mitzi cries. Harry, huddled behind the bushes watches with amusement as Mitzi struggles.

29

Open for Business

B rad and Kim wake early, have a quick breakfast and begin loading the trunk of their car for the first of what is to become several years of attendance at trade shows, antique shows and flea markets where they buy, sell and trade collectible items, mostly vintage watches, clocks and instruments of time from ships, vehicles and airplanes.

Finally, Brad realizes his dream of turning his many hobbies into a business. As the son of an antique dealer, he has an ongoing curiosity about and respect for hand crafted items. As a result, he has knowledge of fine crystal, silver and gold jewelry, exotic wood furniture and antique metal toys. He is also an enthusiastic collector.

From his study of stamps, known as philately, he moved to studying and collecting vintage post cards called deltiology. Because of the geography learned through stamp collecting, he began to study and collect maps, otherwise known as cartography. That led to philography which is autograph collecting. Ephemera represents the collection of paper such as trade cards, greeting and holiday cards, letters, pamphlets, posters and prospectuses. His newest and most favorite area of study is horology, the study of time.

He used his vast knowledge to earn extra money while he worked his way through school by buying and selling antiques and collectibles. Kim admires his intelligence and his patience. That kind of knowledge takes years of study. He's an excellent salesman and he had, no doubt that the combination of salesmanship and knowledge of product would augur well for a successful business. Through osmosis Kim learned quite a bit about the study of time as well and intends to be a great help to him.

As she searches the Internet, she becomes more convinced that Brad should have a virtual store. The concept is new, and she is excited about it but for today her attention is on the grand opening of the antique center and Brad's launch of his new business.

As Brad and Kim load up the trunk with cartons of items for sale, from the corner of her eye she thinks she sees a figure moving through the bushes, but she is in such a rush, she lets it go. It's probably a rabbit.

Just as Kim and Brad are about to get into the car, Pat, in a floppy pink hat and draped in a towel over her bathing suit excitedly approaches. Apparently, she has never seen their garage before.

"How was your swim?" Brad innocently asks.

"Imaginary," Pat swiftly responds.

"Excuse me?" Kim exclaims.

"Something awful happened. The pool's half empty and there's chlorine all over the place. It's all roped off."

"What happened?" Kim demands.

Pat cranes her neck to the point where they think she is going to hurt herself. Ever the gossip, she scans their shelves and takes inventory while breathlessly giving them an account of poor Mitzi's experience at the pool.

"From what I hear, Mitzi went to the pool early for her swim before class. When she saw the pool was almost empty, she went to the filter room to shut off the pumps and was overcome by chlorine fumes. She passed out after screaming for help and someone called 911. She's in the hospital."

"How horrible!" Kim states.

"How could that happen?" Brad wonders out loud.

"Lennard thinks someone messed with the backwash thingy and ransacked the filter room. There were containers of chlorine all over the floor. The pool is closed indefinitely!" Pat adds.

"We hope she's okay," Kim says.

"Yeah, me, too," Pat answers.

"By the way," she continues, "sorry I can't make the opening. I saw the flyer on the bulletin board, but then it was gone, and frankly I forgot the date."

"Another time," Brad says patiently.

"Yes, another time. I knew you would understand." Pat's relieved.

Brad places his arm around Kim. "You'll have to excuse us. We've got a long day ahead of us."

"Yes," Kim adds. "Today is just the first day. It's going to be a long weekend. It's so exciting."

They hug and kiss.

Pat gazes for a moment. "You two really love each other, don't you!"

Kim took her hand. "You know we do."

"I got a pie in the oven. And I am making shish kabob for tonight. Salaam Alechem. Why don't you two come by for dinner? You're not going to cook after a long day of work, are you?"

Brad and Kim look at each other and agree. With all the preparations, they neglected to plan their dinner. Kim is thrilled that Pat no longer sees her as a competitor for Harry Gellis' attention.

"That would be wonderful, but I have no idea what time we will be home," Brad says.

"Not to worry. Whenever you get here, we'll eat. It will be fun. I'll make a nice salad and a surprise dessert."

"We really appreciate that. I completely forgot about dinner." Kim was embarrassed and grateful at the same time. Pat is becoming a friend; she is already a nice neighbor.

"Thanks. 'See you later. Bye," Brad and Kim say in unison.

As they drive away, Pat waves, turns and walks across the street to her home. Kim looks back to wave and thinks she sees Pat stop and stare at the bushes in front of their home. She assumes Pat must have seen the same rabbit as she.

"I read about a wonderful chocolate store on the Net that stays open late. We can stop by on the way home for a gift for her," Kim assures Brad. "Yes, that would be fine." Brad is distracted.

She touches him lightly on the arm.

"Well, today is the first day of your new career," she encourages Brad.

He just smiles, relaxes and puts on the radio. Off they go to the antique center.

Harry's been hiding in the bushes. He heard Pat invite the Wolfs for dinner. He has a plan but first he's going to pay a visit. He peeks out from the bushes, makes sure no one is watching and tiptoes to the back of the Wolfs' home. He dons shoe covers, rubber gloves and disarms the alarm system, the controls of which are in a metal box on the side of the house.

"I got one just like you at home. A jumper wire here, a crossed wire there," he murmurs.

The indicator lamp on the alarm goes off. He picks the back-door lock.

"Open sesame!" Harry declares.

He enters the house and takes a self-guided tour around each room.

"Honey, I'm home!" he calls out to no one.

Harry takes his time moving slowly through each room, touching the furniture, opening closets and drawers.

When Harry reaches the master bedroom, he finds Kim's new lingerie folded neatly on the bed. He takes the panties, rubs them on his face and stuffs them in his pocket.

"Oooh, souvenir."

Across the street, Pat removes a smoldering pie from her oven. She fans the smoke and opens her side door to clear the air. As she lifts the lid of her garbage pail and dumps the pie into it, she looks up and sees Harry walk away from Brad and Kim's house. For a moment their eyes meet. Harry puts his forefinger to his lips to indicate silence, then wiggles it at her as if to threaten her. Frightened and flustered, Pat scurries back inside her house and locks her doors.

30
Antique Center Grand Opening

The air crackles with excitement. The building is new, freshly painted and glistens in the morning sun. "Grand Opening" banners line the street leading to the entrance. As Brad and Kim drive up to the parking area, they acknowledge other antique dealers. People of all ages and backgrounds unload boxes, display cases and inventory from their autos, trucks and vans. They share rolling carts and help each other lug their goods into the center. Part of the parking lot is roped off for mobile homes. Kim and Brad admire those who drive cross country for a three day show and live in the trailers.

Brad parks as close to the loading platform as possible. They hang their identification badges around their necks and join the throng in unloading their wares for sale. The space inside is vast, light and bright. Several rows of six-foot tables line the center of the hall. Booths are set up against the walls. The energy is frenetic as 300 dealers flit around preparing their display spaces for the ten o'clock opening to the public. For certified dealers, the show opens at nine o'clock.

Kim and Brad move rapidly to post their sign and arrange their collectibles, antiques and watches for display. Kim cleans the locked cases which will house the most valuable watches and collectibles. Brad displays their items for sale. Kim makes sure everything is tagged appropriately and sets up her little "office" space with a calculator, pens, pads, tags, business cards, etc. She oversees the sales and the record-keeping while Brad 'works the floor' for items to buy, sell and trade. It is common for dealers to bargain with each other before, during and after each show. Kim's excited and having fun; Brad is focused, tense.

Kim places water, sandwiches and snacks in the corner and is just about to sit when the dealers arrive. Time to stand up, no time to sit. Many dealers like to shop for thirty cents on the dollar, so Brad is very wise in his pricing. She knows which items she can discount and although she admittedly is not as adept as Brad as a negotiator, she makes sure with codes how much she can bargain with the customers.

Brad returns to the booth for water. As Kim is reorganizing items for the third time, a lovely Native American woman approaches. She is about forty, dressed in a knee length cotton dress called a manta, which is fastened at the right shoulder, leaving the left shoulder bare. She looks like she stepped out of a movie set and in her deer skin moccasins floats gracefully into the booth. Her thick black hair is tied in two long pigtails. She wears unique silver earrings and bracelets and several strands of polished beads around her neck. She extends her hand and said simply,

"I see I am blessed with pleasant neighbors."

"As are we," Brad replies and shakes her hand.

"Hello, I am Kim, and this is my husband, Brad."

"My name is Poli Mana. It means Butterfly Girl, but everyone calls me Peggy," She says softly.

Brad begins to fidget.

He addresses Poli Mana, "It is very nice to meet you and I wish you good luck today."

He turns toward Kim and begs, "Honey, do you mind? I need to network."

"Of course not." She kisses him and sends him off with love. "Go! Take all the time you need."

Brad takes off like a thoroughbred and visits as many booths containing watches as he can in the remaining hours.

Poli Mana stays with Kim. Kim looks into her lovely face and says, "You have such a beautiful name. May I call you Poli Mana rather than Peggy?"

"I'd be honored," she replies. Then she adds. "You and your husband, so symbiotic. Yet he carries some sadness in those adoring eyes."

"Are you a psychic?" Kim inquires.

"My people believe that all things in the world have two forms, the physical object and it's spiritual counterpart."

Kim digests that knowledge.

"What are you doing in this business?" Kim inquires.

"I represent a Native American Co-op. We use our crafts to promote cross-cultural understanding."

Later in the day, in a quiet moment, Poli Mana invites Kim to her booth and shows her the Navaho woven blankets, Iroquois wood carvings, Zuni pottery and the Hopi Kachina dolls, pottery and baskets.

"I can feel the pride in every one of these items," Kim notes.

"Yes. They are all hand made," Poli Mana replies.

Poli Mana picks up a Kachina doll and hands it to Kim.

"I was named after this Kachina doll, Butterfly Girl. It's made from cottonwood root. They represent benevolent spirits and are given to children at certain times of the year."

"She's beautiful."

"We believe that Kachina dolls have the power to help us in our lives."

"I've been reading the history of Arizona tribes on the Internet, none of which I learned in school," Kim was embarrassed to say.

Poli Mana just smiles knowingly and with no hint of anger she echoes Lennard and states, "American History was written for White Eyes with not much regard for our truth.

"My parents taught me that the truth always come forth and claims its rightful place; one person at a time, one day at a time," Kim commented.

Poli Mana smiled broadly and handed her a business card.

"Perhaps you and Brad would like to come to a flea market near where I live. Give me a call."

Kim places the card in her pocket and promises herself to discuss it with Brad.

Just before dusk, Brad and Kim pack up and load their car with new merchandise. It has been a long day; they are tired and hungry and eager to return home. Kim calls Pat to let her know they are on their way home.

They stop by the chocolate shop Kim read about which sells chocolate sculptures. They are gorgeous works of art, smell heavenly and taste delicious. They buy Pat sculptured flowers in dark chocolate, milk chocolate and white chocolate and merrily head home, singing along with the car radio.

31

Harry's Revenge, Pat Pays

Pat spent most of the day planning a quiet dinner with Kim and Brad whenever they return home. She sets her backyard table with colored plastic plates, matching cups and plasticware for three and fusses with the brightly patterned pillows and cushions. Tiki lights burn around her back patio, enclosed on three sides by bamboo curtains. She's proud and happy and all looks perfect. She turns on her gas barbecue and while it heats up, she goes back into the kitchen to continue assembling all the ingredients for her meal. As promised, Pat prepares a salad, her shish kabob and a cinnamon apple pie.

Harry hid in the bushes in front of the Wolf's home in the morning and heard Pat offer to make dinner for Kim and Brad. He's been lurking around Pat's house watching her as evening nears. When Pat returns to her kitchen, sure that no one will notice, Harry sneaks into her backyard and turns off the barbecue. He turns on the gas full blast. There is a hissing sound. He absconds with the control knob.

Pat nudges the door open with her knee and carries the platter of shish kabobs to the patio. WHAM!! The barbecue explodes. The bamboo curtains catch fire and the patio fills with smoke. The door knocks Pat to the ground. Blood gushes from her head.

Neighbors quickly put out the fire, drag Pat away from the patio and alert the authorities. Fire, police and rescue vehicles are quick to arrive and fill the street. Surrounded by Randi, a paramedic and neighbors, Pat holds her bandaged head.

32

What Happened to Pat?

Just as Brad and Kim arrive on their block, they are prevented from driving to their home. They park down the street, hurry to the scene and rush to Pat's side. They are horrified.

"My God, Pat, what happened?" Kim begs.

"My barbecue blew up! The kitchen door wacked me in the head. I am afraid dinner's ruined."

"That's not important," Brad says almost dismissively. He turns to Randi who seems to be in charge. "We are the Wolfs. What can we do to help?"

"My ears are still ringing," Pat laments.

Randi throws up his hands in defeat and declares, "She absolutely refuses to go to the hospital. She even signed a waiver to that effect.

"But don't you think you should get checked out?" Kim urges.

"No, no, no. I won't go to the hospital. People die there," Pat affirms.

"I suggest she stay with friends – someone needs to keep an eye on her. She's had a rough time," Randi speaks up.

Brad and Kim say in unison, "She can stay with us."

Brad helps Pat to her feet. "No, no, no. I am alright really. I'll stay here and if I need anything, I'll call you."

"We have plenty of room," Kim conveys.

Stubbornly, Pat asserts, "I insist on sleeping in my own bed."

Everybody backs off. Brad and Kim accompany Pat inside her home. Brad is captivated by the walls in her living room. There are hats of every color, shape and fabric hanging on posts tacked to the walls. It is an awesome sight.

Pat asks for tea and crackers. Brad prepares the tea and crackers while Kim guides Pat to the bathroom to help her prepare for bed. Pat is able to digest the tea and crackers easily and seems to relax. She is tired, so they escort her to the bedroom, admire another wall of hats and make sure Pat is comfortable and safe in bed. Pat gives Kim an extra key and Kim promises to check in with her in the morning before they go back to the antique center.

The police cars, fire trucks and ambulance leave the scene; neighbors disperse. With Pat's permission, Randi, the fire chief, a chubby man about forty-five and Christine Lord, a beautiful tall, red-headed, thirty something woman, the community based police officer stay behind to investigate the scene. The only damage is to the patio area. Brad and Kim stay with Pat until she falls asleep.

Brad and Kim wait on the patio while, Randi, the fire chief and Christine finish their investigation and fill out reports, take photos of the damage and collect debris. It is getting quite late. Kim and Brad are eager to lock up and get home.

Christine inquires of the fire chief, "What was it, chief, the wind?"

"At this point I don't know how else it might have happened. It's been pretty gusty."

"She could have been killed," Kim laments.

Randi, the Fire Chief and Christine complete their work and leave the premises.

"First the pool, now this. What a freaky day," Brad sighs.

Brad retrieves their car and parks it in the garage. It is quite late when they arrive home. They unload the car and carry boxes towards the house. They are both distressed and fatigued.

As they approach the house, Brad notices something amiss on the alarm key pad.

"You didn't set the alarm right this morning," he scolds.

She is so damned tired, all she could say is, "I thought I did."

"Well, the pressure mat wasn't activated. You have to do that separately every time. When we go out for the day, I'd like it set!" Brad is agitated.

"Then you set it!" Kim angrily reacts.

"Don't get mad at me!" Brad raises his voice.

"Then don't give me orders. I am sure I set it!"

"Forget it."

Silently, they enter the house and tote the boxes to the office. Brad exits quickly, Kim stays behind and organizes the checks and cash. She turns on the computer and while it takes its time to start up, she notices her writer's magazine. As she moves it aside, the King of Hearts card falls out of it, Harry Gellis' calling card.

Kim panics. "How did the card get into my magazine?" she mumbles softly. Then she remembers the tussle on the shuttle and realizes he must have slipped it in without her knowledge. She recoils in disgust.

"What a week! I can hear Dr. Craig telling me to stay calm and avoid all stress," she giggles cynically.

As she smiles at that, she hears Brad in the kitchen moving pots around. She's forgotten they haven't eaten anything.

"Hey, honey. I'm making soup. Lentil okay?" Brad calls out.

She shoves the card in her desk drawer. The computer hasn't booted up yet, so she joins Brad in the kitchen.

They automatically fall into each other's arms and hug tight.

"I'm sorry I was short with you," Brad confesses.

"I'm sorry I yelled at you. It's okay. We're both exhausted. Thanks for making the soup." Kim is grateful. Neither of them has much of an appetite and it is getting quite late. They have the soup and crackers and it is enough. They eye Pat's chocolate but decide against eating it so late and put it away, laughing. They have two long days to get through at the antique center.

Still unsettled, Brad begins to pace and pulls on his hair. Kim has never seen him do that before. She puts her arms around him.

"What's wrong?" She is uneasy.

"It was a dismal day as far as business is concerned. I thought I would do much better," he complains.

"You're too hard on yourself. You did fine for your first day. I'll add it all up and give you the total."

"You think it was alright?"

"I think we made a profit. Besides, Poli Mana told me about a flea market near where she lives," she soothes.

"Where?"

"Sedona. Why don't we go?"

"That's about two to three hours from here. Do you think it will be worth it?"

"Yes. You might make some connections. If nothing else, the scenery will be worth seeing."

Kim is excited about going to Sedona. She had hoped they would make the trip someday. The photos of the towering red rocks, unusual sculptures against magnificent skies and deep canyons do not capture the natural beauty seen by one's own eyes.

She has another reason for wanting to go. Sedona is the home of a metaphysical phenomenon known as the vortex; it is a whirling mass of energy pulling power to its center. It is known for its power spots and offers guided tours and spiritual quests for relaxation and tranquility. She wants to explore the area for healing. She is exploring alternative healing methods.

"If you think it's worth it, we'll go," Brad agrees.

Kim is elated. She kisses him and plans it out in her head.

"Great, I'll tell Poli Mana in the morning." She is excited.

"Let's have some tea and go to bed," Brad suggests.

The mood lifts. They are tired but optimistic. Just a cup of tea and off to bed.

Brad arranges the cups and saucers and sets the tea kettle to boil. Kim goes to the refrigerator for milk and removes a gallon of milk. The tea kettle whistles. She drops the gallon of milk and it spills all over the floor.

"Damn it, Brad! Why did you buy a gallon size?" she yells in frustration.

"I saved seventy-five cents," he answers innocently.

Exasperated, she cries, "Your seventy-five cents are now all over the floor!"

She hobbles quickly for the mop. The tea kettle whistle screams louder. Brad runs after her and tries to take the mop from her hands.

"I'll do it," he blurts.

"Don't bother. You've done enough!" She is furious.

"Let me help you," he begs.

"Leave me alone!" she shouts.

Kim is blinded by emotion, a mixture of fear, embarrassment, anger and frustration. She slips and falls against the gallon of milk spilling more of what was left. The teapot whistle is getting louder. She just sits on the floor, unhurt but stunned into silence.

"Please let me help you!" Brad pleads.

He attempts to help her up. She pushes him away and manages to crawl to a dry place and with the help of a sturdy chair, hauls herself up and sits in the chair.

"You're the one who needs help. Use your brains and look at things from my perspective," she demands.

Panicked, Brad pleas, "What's happening to you? Make me understand!"

"My hands don't work, my legs don't work, the pain is maddening and all you can think of is saving a lousy seventy-five cents!"

At that point, the tea kettle screech is ear piercing at its highest pitch. Brad finally shuts it down and begins to cry repeating over and over, "I'm so sorry."

"No. The apology is mine. I am the one who's sorry, so very sorry. I should have told you. The doctor warned me these things would happen and that there would be great challenges ahead. I promise I will do better. Just know that I adore you." It is her turn to cry.

Although Brad and Kim apologize to each other and make peace, they are emotionally raw. Each of them avoids talking about the spilt milk.

They hug for a long time and sleep holding hands through the night. They are both terrified of what lay ahead. Kim vows to never let a scene like that happen again. She thinks the noblest thing to do is to give him his freedom and let him go. She weeps through the night as she plans to release Brad from their marriage.

The next morning, Kim rises early, fixes breakfast, packs a lunch and snacks and prepares for the second day of selling. She looks out the window and sees Pat's lights on. She calls Pat to see how she is and asks if she can stop by before she and Brad leave for the day. Pat agrees. Kim goes across the street, while Brad is asleep.

"Pat, you look better. I want to make sure you are okay before we leave for the day."

"Where are you going?" Pat implores. She seems perturbed.

Patiently, Kim explains, "It's the antique center grand opening. Brad and I have to work this weekend. "

"Why?" Pat challenges.

"Because Brad started his new business."

"Oh," Pat is clearly bewildered.

Pat, who can I call to come and stay with you?"

"Why?" Pat asks, childlike.

"You had a nasty accident. I'd like someone to check in on you, prepare lunch for you and maybe dinner."

"Why?"

"Because I have to leave, and I want to make sure you are alright."

Pat roams around befuddled. Kim notices a telephone book beside Pat's telephone on a small table. "I'll call Carla."

Kim returns home. Brad is eating breakfast and rushing through it.

"Slow down. We have plenty of time." Kim reminds him.

"No, we don't! We've got to get to the parking lot early. The watch guys are hungry. We're all looking for the same merchandise - Rolexes, Pateks, and chronographs. They told me they buy, sell and trade on the hoods of their cars and out of their trunks even before the antique center opens. Did you notice the international trade? I don't want to miss anything."

"Well, then, let's go. I'm ready!"

There is a rhythm to these events. The buyers, mostly men disappear into the morass of exhibit tables and booths, bent over with loops and lights attached to their heads and glasses examining the minute details of each watch, pocket watch, instrument or part such as dial, case, hands, movement and original box and papers.

Some of the dealers are table hogs, spreading out their elbows, preventing others from looking at the merchandise until they are finished. If the tables are next to each other, sometimes the sellers "accidentally" move their merchandise onto their neighbor's space pushing the boundaries of manners and good business behavior. The pros are knowledgeable, make snap decisions in seconds worth thousands of dollars and move quickly to the next potential deal.

Kim waits while one of the international dealers reviews Brad's merchandise. He has just landed at Phoenix Airport and came directly to the show without sleep. He is dressed like a student in jeans, a short sleeve shirt and carries a knapsack. He absent-mindedly leaves the knapsack on the table and swiftly disappears in the crowd. Kim holds it for him and dispatches Brad to find him. The knapsack contains several thousand dollars in cash and high end watches for sale. He is so grateful to retrieve it all intact he gives Brad the first preview. Brad buys several watches and that seals an ongoing friendship for many years and gives Brad a reputation as a trustworthy dealer.

During a lull in the activity Kim keeps in touch with Carla and is pleased to hear Pat is resting, eating well and doing fine.

By the third day, Brad is happy and comfortable in his element. The last two days of the Antique center's opening weekend mirrors the first. Sales are spotty, they break even, and Kim thinks that is a good thing; Brad disagrees.

Kim spends the rest of the week researching places for Brad to buy merchandise as well as places to sell what he has. Then she focuses on their upcoming Sedona trip but first they have to figure out what to wear to Mitzi's 1970's party.

33

Harry Moves from Annoying to Stalking

Kim spends the afternoon in the shopping center. She goes to the department store looking for a blouse with a big bold print. She has high boots and palazzo pants. Brad has large sunglasses and an old paisley print shirt. They're set for the party.

She picks up Brad's shirts from the cleaners and as she pays, she sees the reflection of Harry's face in the mirror. She turns instantly to catch him; in a flash, he's gone. Is she seeing things?

Her next stop is at the bank and as she stands in line, Harry passes by the window and waves. She ignores the wave and thinks perhaps he is doing his errands as well. She gives it no more thought until she is at the hair salon sitting in the chair getting her hair trimmed. There are three customers taken care of by three hairdressers.

Harry enters and turns on the charm.

"Hello ladies. What will you charge me to make me more handsome? I have a hot date I need to impress."

"Our list of prices is posted here over the desk, sir," answers the youngest of the three women stylists. I can take your name – there is a fifteen minute wait time."

Harry scans the list of prices. "Twelve dollars for a senior haircut? What a rip-off! Can't you do better than that!"

The young woman is flabbergasted. "Sir, these are our prices. I could get in trouble if I didn't charge you right."

"No coupons? No discount for residents of Pima Vista?" He turns towards Kim. "What do you think, pretty lady?"

"I think you should shop somewhere else." The young hairdresser is relieved. The other two giggle.

Harry is miffed. His face flushes, lips thin out, eyes widen with an icy stare. His demeanor changes from charming to alarming. He bangs his fist on the counter and in a boisterous voice, demands, "I want to see the manager! Now!"

The atmosphere darkens. Fear grips the young girl. The other two hairdressers stop their work and stand mute. Kim is startled and afraid as are the other two women customers.

The young girl dials the phone and whispers into it.

"Well?" Harry booms. "Anyone gonna help me here?"

The young girl hands Harry the phone and stutters, "my manager is on the line."

Kim whispers to her hairdresser, pays in cash, gathers her belongings and prepares to leave.

Harry takes the phone and listens intently. "Yeah, well you run a lousy establishment!" He bangs the phone in its cradle.

His attention turns to Kim as she heads towards the door. His mood lightens. "If you're finished, I'll walk you home."

"No, thanks." Kim moves as quickly as she can and goes to the supermarket. She has no idea where Harry is and focuses on her shopping list, when Harry pops up behind the lettuce in the produce section.

She is flabbergasted. These meetings are not a coincidence.

At her wits end, she quietly asks, "What do you want from me?"

"You know, wink, wink, nod, nod," he sneers.

"Mr. Gellis, there are many women here who would be delighted if you would call them for a date."

"Nah, did you ever see them naked? They're wrinkly and ugly. They don't have your youth, your class. 'See ya' soon, cutie." Before she can react, he is gone.

Kim's new assignment as a volunteer is to work with the city attorney to clean up some of the outdated language on traffic laws. She has access to his law books and with his permission, checks current laws on stalking.

34

The 70's Party - Bell Bottoms and Burritos

The party at the Clubhouse went forward as planned by Mitzi who recovered well enough not only to attend but to take charge.

She is a vision dressed in white and gold from head to toe. She wears high heeled white patent leather boots with gold buckles under bell bottom slacks, topped by a light knit scoop necked blouse tied below the waist. A silky gold toned scarf is wrapped around her curly brunette hair and tied it in such a way that one side of the scarf flows over her right shoulder. Her gold tone chandelier earrings match her thin gold tone bracelets. She wears gold eye shadow.

One hundred and fifty people are expected to attend. Mitzi in her zealousness, over decorates the room with ads and magazine covers circa 1970's. Crepe paper flowers are taped to whatever space is left on the walls. Mitzi's taste borders on school child arts and crafts depictions. Kim assumes she operated with a small budget. Her taste could be best described as kitschy.

On each table, burritos, chips, pretzels and soft drinks surround photos of John Travolta in his signature white suit from "Saturday Night Fever," Farah Fawcett in her red one piece bathing suit, Marlon Brando as "The Godfather," Burt Reynolds in tight jeans, western shirt and a cowboy hat and the cast of "Saturday Night Live" in handmade frames with glued-on decorations. Folding chairs are placed around the wooden dance floor. A disco ball hangs from the ceiling. The disco music is loud, the mood light.

Several people get into the spirit and dress for the occasion. There are a variety of leisure suits, pant suits, jumpsuits and track suits, granny dresses, bell bottoms, polyester and platform shoes. One group of ladies, wear wigs illustrating the hairstyles of the era – made famous by actors, musicians and sports figures such as the feather cut, the wedge, the Afro, the shag and straight hair with bangs.

Carla drifts by, nose buried in a book. Kim calls to her twice before she hears her. She introduces Brad to Carla.

"'Nice to meet you, Carla. What are you reading?" Brad inquires.

Carla is confounded by Brad's question. She looks at the book in her hand as though she didn't realize it was there. She quickly thumbs through the pages until she finds what she wants.

"Watches, watches, no watchmakers." She repeats. Now, where did I see that information about toilets?"

"Toilets?" Kim repeats. "What do toilets have to do with watches?" Brad smiles.

Carla is excited now. "Yes, yes, yes. Here it is. Are you aware that in 1775 a Scottish watchmaker living in London named Alexander Cumming was responsible for improving the flushing toilet?"

"Do you know how?" Brad challenges.

Carla is stumped. "No."

"Cumming was not only a watchmaker, but an inventor of instruments as well. He developed the S-trap or U or J shaped pipe trap which retained water permanently within the bowl." He continues, "But the first flushing toilet was invented for Queen Elizabeth the First, I believe, in the 1500's," Brad lectures.

"Wait a minute!" Carla implores. She flips through several pages and reads aloud, "Queen Elizabeth the First's godson, Sir John Harrington invented the flushing toilet for her in 1596 and wrote a book about it with directions on how to build one which was largely ignored. Oh, I get it -- the John!" She exclaims.

They all laugh. Carla marks the passage for a future reread.

Brad adds, "If I am correct, Queen Elizabeth the First also

received a wrist watch from someone named Dudley, but I think it was described as an arm watch."

"Hmm," Carla mused. "Most interesting, most interesting. I will have to look that up," she mumbles as she wanders away.

"How did you know that?" Kim asks Brad.

"You are not the only one who reads," Brad intonates.

"I feel a Scrabble game coming," Kim challenges.

A quartet of neighbor musicians play "The Hustle." Pat recovered from her head wound quickly and is eager to see and be seen. Dressed in her "Annie Hall" costume, beige pants, black vest and white long sleeved man tailored shirt with a long striped tie, she topped it off with a beige floppy hat. Energetic Pat skips to the center of the dance floor and performs a spirited solo. She tries coaxing the guests to participate but all are satisfied to watch her and marvel or gossip about her dance skills. Kim admires her freedom to just be and thoroughly enjoys the show.

Brad and Kim clap enthusiastically as Pat finishes her act, bows to the musicians and then to the audience. The applause is spontaneous and well-deserved.

Pat glows in the attention and leaves the dance floor slightly out of breath. She waves to Kim and Brad and begins to walk toward them. Brad offers to bring them drinks.

"I'll be right back." He kisses Kim on the cheek and walks towards the beverage table.

Harry Gellis blocks Pat's path. Harry teases her and moves from side to side preventing her from her from reaching Kim.

Hands on hips, Pat demands, "either we dance, or you get out of my way."

"Hey, I heard about the fire," Harry offers.

"Thanks for your concern. You could have called," Pat scolds.

"If you were as hot in the bedroom as you are on the barbecue, I might have," Harry maligned.

Pat disregards the clumsy and rude insult and feigns right while he moves right to cut her off again. This time, she scoots left around him and into the safety of Kim's arms. Brad has returned with the drinks but missed the Harry/Pat tussle. Kim explains that Pat is tired and needs to sit for a while. Brad understands.

Just then Mitzi grabs the microphone, congratulates Pat on her exhibition and welcomes all to the dance floor. Brad leaves to retrieve a drink for Pat while she and Kim watch others on the dance floor.

"Harry is such a jerk. I don't know what I saw in him," Pat confides.

"How long has he lived here?" Kim asks.

"Oh, about a year and a half ago he moved in with his wife or was it two years ago? I only saw her once. Apparently, she was quite ill and then I heard she passed. They pretty much kept to themselves, so no one really knew she was gone until Harry started showing up at the single's club. He was very popular – not bad looking don't you think? Well anyway, he's quite a flirt and at times can be charming and funny. Frankly, I'm disappointed. I'm looking for a companion and thought we had a good thing going. But I was wrong," Pat said sadly.

"Why?" Kim urged.

"He can be quite rough at times – physically, verbally and emotionally. He's got a dark soul," she said knowingly. She added with a wink, "and a bad wig." They both smiled at that tidbit which lightened the mood.

"Does he have any children?" Kim probed.

"Mitzi says no. She knows him the longest. But I think he has a nephew or a business manager or something who takes care of his finances. I'm not sure."

Kim tried to remember the time she saw Harry and the Suit on the tourist bus. She could only hear fragments of their conversation; the Suit could have been a business manager.

Something just doesn't feel right about Harry. While he seems to be so well-known and obvious in his behavior, she has the feeling there is more to him than just an annoying old man. She just can't put her finger on it.

The band-leader takes the microphone and announces, "And now for those warm and fuzzy memories of music and dance that defines romance." The band plays a slow dance.

Harry approaches Kim and Pat. "Hey Kim or should I say Cinderella. How about a slow dance before I turn into a kumquat?" She is quick to reply, "No, thanks!"

Harry pulls her by the hand. They hear a crack. She recoils in pain and pulls her hand back massaging it. "Ow! I said No! Why don't you leave me alone?"

Brad, drink in hand rushes over and hands the drink to Pat. She stands silently holding the drink. Brad hovers over Kim. Harry stays where he is chuckling to himself.

"Are you alright?" Brad asks Kim with concern.

Before she can respond, Harry interjects, "A woman's tragedy – a broken nail."

"I'm fine, Brad, really. It's a broken blood vessel. I see the doctor Monday morning."

Brad grew six inches taller in her eyes as he fearlessly confronts Harry straight on.

"Who are <u>you</u>?" Brad interrogates, emphasis on you.

Harry turns on the charm, reaches out to shake Brad's hand and introduces himself.

"Harry Gellis, your neighborly, nearby neighbor."

Brad looks at Kim and winks and nods knowingly. "I see."

"I'm alright, Brad. Mr. Gellis is looking for a dancing partner," she says as calmly as she can.

Brad takes charge. "Sir. My wife doesn't dance and if she could it would be only with me."

"Ah, call me Harry. After all, the best way to enjoy a beautiful garden is to live next door to one and cultivate your neighbor." Harry smiles through gritted teeth. He is enjoying the joust.

"Look for someone else to sprout with. Good night!" Brad says with authority and turns his back on Harry. Harry shrugs, gives a little salute to all and meanders across the room.

Both Brad and Kim focus on Pat. Pat is frozen in place, eyes glazed over with a blank stare. She looks lost. Kim has witnessed this before when picking up the mail. She met Pat and while they were chit chatting about the weather, Pat was in the middle of a sentence and she just stopped – talking, moving. She froze. It lasted only a few seconds, but Kim is becoming increasingly concerned about her.

Brad helps Kim to her feet and suggests, "Let's go home. Pat? Do you want us to take you home?"

Pat snaps out of her daze and drinks the water. "What?"

"Brad and I are going home. Do you want to come with us?" Kim says gently.

"Home? Now? No, thanks. The night's young. I'm NMO," she chirps.

"NMO?" Brad is confused.

"Yeah, NMO. I'm Not Missing Out!" she squeals.

Her energy returns. She looks like she is about to dance again. Brad and Kim wave their goodbyes and leave.

Mitzi in dark glasses runs after them. "Where are you two going so early?"

Kim introduces Brad to Mitzi. "Brad, meet Mitzi, our activities director."

Mitzi turns on her charm. "Well hello Brad. So nice to finally meet you. I feel as though I know all about you just from your recyclables."

Brad is perplexed. "I'll explain later," Kim assures him.

"The night is young. We're going to have contests and prizes…" Mitzi prattles on.

"You will have to excuse us. I have an early meeting tomorrow. Kim tells me how hard you work, so let me take this opportunity to compliment you. We had fun."

They walk towards the exit of the clubhouse.

Mitzi's whole demeanor changes. She calls after them, "It was Harry, wasn't it? I saw him talking to you. I'm going to kill that bastard. He ruins everything!"

Before they have a chance to respond, Mitzi turns around quickly and walks towards Harry.

Wagging a finger at Harry, Mitzi berates him. "You listen to me, Harry Gellis. I worked too hard on this party to have you scare off the guests."

"What are you? The house Detective? Wanna put that finger to good use while you frisk me?" he teases.

"Have a drink and cool off," Mitzi advises.

"Good idea!" Harry exclaims.

Just then, Carla ambles by, focused on a book in one hand, drink in the other. Harry grabs the drink out of Carla's hand and gulps it down.

"Ugh! Somebody put pineapple juice in your pineapple juice." He spits it out on the floor and returns the cup to Carla. "You know, Carla, you should do some chest exercises. You're built like a revolving door – no knobs."

Carla seems flummoxed, throws the cup away and rushes to the exit. Mitzi stomps her foot, turns her back and seizes several napkins off a nearby table. She cleans the floor where he left his spittle, then marches away in a huff. Harry laughs, then glares at Brad and Kim. Brad places his arm around Kim, and they leave.

"I see what you mean. He is a strange character. Just stay away from him," Brad counsels.

"I will," she meekly replies.

She thinks to herself, "How am I going to stay away from a man who is stalking me? Do I tell Brad? Of course not. He has so much on his mind worrying about my health, his new business and just acclimating himself to Arizona. I know he misses Manhattan but is making a vigorous effort to have it all work out."

She thought of her plan to release him from their marriage which breaks her heart, but she feels it is the noblest thing she can do. But when and how and where would she go? She would have to get him set up first successfully in business, make sure he is happy in his new home and that he is financially comfortable.

How could she leave this wonderful, loving man who she adores? Does she really think letting him go would protect him? Perhaps it would be best if she focuses on healing rather than being sick and dying. She makes a solemn promise that night to never leave Brad.

Kim has a new resolve. She feels empowered and creates a plan in her head. Harry is a nuisance, easily dismissed; she has more important things to do. She can't wait to get home to her computer. She is going to prove the doctors wrong.

35

There's More to Medicine Than Pills

At the time Kim is diagnosed there are no support groups available to them, no other patients with whom to share information. Her doctor, also a researcher told her she was only the third patient diagnosed with Takayasu's Arteritis, a rare form of vasculitis in that hospital. When she asked him about the other two patients, sadly, he reported that they died, but one woman went past menopause so there is hope, and Kim eagerly looks forward to the experience of menopause. Kim realizes she is pretty much on her own.

Occasionally she and Brad attended meetings for patients with other auto-immune diseases like Lupus and Scleroderma. She discovered it really doesn't matter what the disease is called. All who are affected by ongoing illnesses have to learn how to live with their respective conditions. It is as important for the patient as well as the care-giver to be educated and supported.

The immediate objective is to stay out of a wheelchair. She used one a few times back in New York and hates seeing the world from a seated position.

The first time she used a wheelchair was when she and Brad visited her favorite place in Manhattan, the Metropolitan Museum of Art. It was her sanctuary, but she could no longer walk the great halls. So, one Sunday they rented a wheelchair. An old-fashioned wheelchair that had to be pushed. Ever the gallant man, Brad assured her he was fine pushing her around the museum and did so joyfully but quietly singing in her ear, Rollover Beethoven, Rock and Roll All Night and Rollin on the River which amused Kim and took away the growing sadness.

The first mishap was when they took the elevator. Brad wheeled her in but since there was no room to turn her around, she faced the back wall while everyone else faced front, which struck her as humorous. While attempting to stifle her laughter, a few giggles escaped which seemed mystify the other passengers.

Brad leaned over and whispered, "Did you enjoy the wall art?" and she burst into laughter. When he backed her out of the elevator it was clear where she had been, but she was unable to see where she was going, so she smiled and waved as they left. Some people gawked some bowed their heads. Kim never understood why it made people uncomfortable.

While meandering through one of the exhibits, a well-meaning but ignorant docent bent down to greet them and screamed in Kim's ear. For some reason, she equated her impaired mobility with being hard of hearing, which made Kim laugh. That happened more than once.

Brad, ever the curious sort parked her and was so engrossed in lovely pottery, that he didn't realize he left her in the middle of an aisle. Unable to manipulate the chair on her own, right then and there she decided against purchasing a wheelchair.

Her heating pad is a dear ally. Topical creams work sporadically. Ice, wraps and braces are helpful as are compression stockings, wedges and pillows. And of course, a sensible diet and daily exercise either in bed or on terra firma.

Up until this point, the only treatment she has been offered is a series of medications to control blood pressure, prevent strokes and ease the pain. But these medications have a series of effects beyond those used for treatment as all do, so as a result she's developed other conditions and takes more medicine. She wants better solutions.

She investigates methods of healing in addition to traditional medicine replete with the required pharmaceuticals. Together, Kim and Brad visit bookstores and libraries; Kim digests as many books as she can about health and healing and is open to all forms of traditional medicine as well as naturopathic, holistic, complementary and alternative medicine. It is an interesting time and as they focus on being healthy, as opposed to being ill, anything Kim tries, Brad is right by her side.

She is eager to share her expanding knowledge with Dr. Craig.

36

Harry's Trip to Doctor Craig

The office is crowded. Harry stands by the receptionists' desk randomly flicking ashes from his cigarette. He fills out forms while Sally and Dee chat away, gorging on donuts.

Harry raps on the glass enclosure, papers in hand. Dee opens the window. "Hey, beautiful, where have you been all my life?" Harry says flirtatiously.

Dee, not shy answers, "Well for the first fifty years, I wasn't even born. Please put your cigarette out."

Dee turns away to retrieve a folder. Harry's eyes follow her figure as he jams his lit cigarette into a potted cactus. Harry shakes his hand as if to fan his face and declares, "What a caboose! You're right (cough, cough), bad for you. But it isn't the cough that will carry you off, it's the coffin they carry you off in." He looks around the room for attention. Other patients are not amused.

Harry raps on the glass again. Dee opens the window. "How may I help you?" she asks.

"Well, where it says here on the form "Sex", do I put down yes or no?"

Dee giggles and shuts the window. Some of the patients, half-smile, some appear to be embarrassed.

Kim arrives on time for her appointment. Harry sees her before she sees him.

"Well, here she is – our own little mermaid," he announces.

Kim is horrified. "Why are you here?" she demands.

"Since you look so good with the limp, I figured I'd check out your doctor. So here I am ready for our lunch date," he states proudly.

"We don't have a lunch date," she retorts.

Kim marches into the cubicle where Sally and Dee sit. Startled, they both sit at attention.

"Kim, seething, demands attention. "Now quietly, tell me why that man is here."

Apologetically, Dee stammers in a whisper. "He came by the day after you were here and said you told him to make an appointment today so you could travel together."

"What do you mean he came by?"

"He was in a hurry. He said he forgot Dr. Craig's name and went to all the offices in the building checking to see if you were a patient because you told him to see Dr. Craig! Dee tearfully explains.

"I did nothing of the sort!"

Dee continues. "He insisted he had to see the doctor and when I asked him what was wrong, he said, 'I got pain down there. Got it?' I didn't know how to handle him, so Sally took over. After she introduced herself, she asked him how she could help.

He was very rude and shouted, 'How many broads do I have to tell this to? I got pain, down there. Know what I'm talking about?"

Sally calmed him down and told him 'We're not broads and yes, I know what you are talking about. I can get you in on Monday at two o'clock.'"

"He insisted that you wanted us to make an appointment at the same time as yours, so you could travel together. And that's why Sally scheduled him to come in today." Dee took a long deep breath.

"For your information, that's the man I complained about last week. You know, the one who flirted with a cripple," Kim said.

Sally finally spoke up. "You heard that?" she said with some embarrassment.

"I'm not deaf!" Kim answered.

Sally lowered her head. "I'm so sorry, please accept my apology."

Kim was more angry than frightened. "I will if you can get me out of here another way. I'll need a taxi."

They could all see Harry lingering close to the cubicle straining to hear what was being discussed while pretending to read the forms.

Sally perked up and whispered, "I'll have a taxi waiting for you at the back exit. Stay in the exam room after the doctor leaves; I'll come and get you."

Kim felt better. "Fine, just don't ever book me and "Hot Pants Harry" at the same time again."

"We won't," Sally and Dee replied in unison.

Sally added, "You may see the doctor now."

Kim marched out of the cubicle and passed a curious Harry. He started to say something; she just glared at him and continued toward the examination room.

Harry handed his papers to Dee who placed them in a file folder. Harry relaxed and took a seat. Dee and Sally took turns keeping a watchful eye on Harry.

Sally says thoughtfully, "Franky, I didn't think he was her type. You keep him busy while I get her out of here."

Kim listened intently as Dr. Craig read from her file. "The brain MRI shows no signs of immediate danger."

"When I asked my New York neurologist for more information, he told me, 'To know more, we would have to do an autopsy – don't volunteer.' Sage advice, don't you think?" Dr. Craig isn't quite comfortable with that kind of cynicism.

Kim hopes Dr. Craig will be more forthcoming. "What do you think the swellings mean?" she implores.

"UBOS or unidentified bright objects are an indication of inflammation. Continue the aspirin. You'll be fine," he assures her. "Now, let me see your finger."

Her right forefinger is purple and swollen.

"Ischemia. Interrupted blood supply. The discoloration and swelling are beginning to dissipate – not to worry. Soak it in warm water when you return home."

He makes some notes and continues, "I have to ask. How is your sex life?"

"Like the weather here, hot." They both laugh at her answer. "Sometimes I think it is the only part of me that works well," she adds.

"Good. And how does your husband handle your illness?"

Kim realizes he is creating a behavioral profile and is the only doctor who asked about her husband. She likes that.

"Okay as long as I function. But he panics during the flare-ups."

"Does he know everything?"

"Everything he can absorb. But neither you nor I know everything. He's fragile now and I need to protect him."

"Why do you say he is fragile?"

"He gets angry at the thought of my dying. Add to that he is starting a new business and trying to adjust to the move here from New York – he's having a rough go of it all."

"Have him call me if he has any questions," Dr. Craig says nonchalantly as he makes notes.

Kim thought perhaps she should ask his opinion about letting Brad go. Oh, it was all too much to assimilate. Her head is spinning, but she is glad she has someone with knowledge of the disease who cares about their emotional health.

Dr. Craig writes a prescription and hands it to her.

"More medicine?" she laments.

"I'm increasing your blood pressure medicine. All things considered you are doing fine. Stay relaxed and avoid conflict and stress. Now let me see the list you prepared."

He reviews Kim's alphabetical list of alternative healing methods and gives his opinion.

- Acupressure
- Acupuncture
- Allopathic Medicine
- Alternative Medicine
- Angel Readings
- Aromatherapy
- Art Therapy
- Ayurvedic Medicine
- Biofeedback
- Biomedicine
- Chiropractic Therapy
- Color Therapy
- Complementary Medicine
- Counseling
- Diet Modification
- Electro Magnetic Therapy
- Homeopathy
- Holistic Medicine
- Hypnotherapy
- Integrative Medicine
- Massage Therapy
- Meditation
- Mind, Body Spirit Work
- Music therapy
- Naturopathic Medicine
- Nutritional Therapy
- Palliative Medicine
- Physical Therapy
- Psychic Readings
- Reflexology
- Reiki
- Shiatsu
- Stress Reduction

- Tai Chi
- Vibrational Medicine
- Vitamin Therapy
- Yoga

"There is a good physical therapy program at the local hospital; call Sally and she will set you up."

He continues to read her list. "The only thing I ask is that before you take any over the counter medicines, vitamin or herbal compounds of any kind, clear it with me so I can determine if there are any interactions with your medicines which may be of concern. I have a patient who took an herbal compound with some treated tree bark and she became quite ill. Go slowly and let me know what you are doing. All methods work if you believe they will."

She felt better after the exam and was eager to return home to Brad. As per Sally's instructions, she waited in the exam room after Dr. Craig left.

Meanwhile back in the reception room, Harry is getting antsy. He remains in front of the glass enclosure and is mesmerized by Dee's expanding rear end as she bends over a table to reach some files. He observes Sally, specimen cup in hand as she retrieves Kim from the exam room, hands her the cup and points towards a door at the end of the hall leading to the rear exit. He watches as Kim enters a bathroom.

Turning his attention back to Dee, he quips, "Hey Miss Tight Butt, where are the Jakes?"

Dee turns around in slow motion. "My name is Dee."

"Yeah, whatever. Where are the Jakes?" Harry repeats.

"Jakes?" She echoes.

"Head," Harry states.

"Head?" Dee harps.

Sure that Dee is keeping Harry occupied, Sally slips out of the cubicle, taps gently on the bathroom door and leads Kim out the back way to a waiting taxi.

"John!" An exasperated Harry scoffs.

"John? Oh, you mean bathroom!" Dee taunts, "It's occupied at the moment."

Dee takes her time writing Harry's name on a plastic cup and hands it to Harry. "When the bathroom is free, you'll have to leave a specimen," she instructs.

"You'll have to get me in the mood," Harry shoots back.

"This is not a fertility clinic. Just pee in the cup!" Dee commands.

"Okay, sweetheart, but no peeking."

Sally returns to the cubicle and reviews Harry's papers.

With his papers in hand, Sally approaches Harry. "You did not complete page three."

Harry suspects a ruse. "Mrs. Wolf's been in the bathroom a long time. Maybe she needs another cup."

Ignoring Harry, Sally continues, "And I need you to sign pages four and five."

Ignoring Sally again, Harry suggests, "Maybe she fell in. Shouldn't somebody check?"

Exasperated, Sally orders, "Mr. Gellis. I need you to focus on these forms."

Harry makes a sudden move toward the bathroom. The door is slightly ajar. He kicks it open. The bathroom is empty. He notices the exit door next to it. He pushes it open to the outside. Down the block a taxi is in sight stopped at a red light.

With a hearty laugh he returns to the cubicle and waves his forefinger at the girls and moves towards the front door.

Sally calls after him, "Mr. Gellis, your appointment!"

Harry slaps his forehead and shouts, "I'm healed. It's a miracle. Gotta go tell the Pharisees."

Sally and Dee stand mute as Harry exites.

37

Lennard Speaks to Harry on Kim's Behalf

Kim rushes home and sets the alarm. The doorbell rings. Kim peeks through the peephole, lets Lennard in and quickly resets the alarm.

"I just came by to see if you needed anything," Lennard says.

Distracted, Kim answers, "Yes, yes. I need additional grab bars in the hallway and master bath."

Lennard makes a note. "Are you okay?" he inquires with some concern.

"No! Harry Gellis was waiting for me at my doctor's office."

Almost dismissively, Lennard says, "Maybe he has the same doctor."

"No, no. He lied to the staff and manipulated an appointment to be there the same time as me. He's stalking me!"

Lennard replies calmly, "He's probably just looking for some company."

Kim urges, "Has anyone else complained about him besides Pat's friend Lydia?"

Not wanting to reveal too much, Lennard answers, "We fielded some complaints."

Kim demanded, "Then why don't you get rid of him?"

Lennard ponders that question and says simply, "The people who complained never followed up on their complaints once they met with his business manager, Mr. Grimm."

"I'd like to know more about this so-called business manager!"

Kim was incredulous.

Lennard added, "Whenever Mr. Gellis bends the rules, we call Mr. Grimm and Harry toes the line.

The doorbell rings. Kim checks the peephole and disconnects the alarm. She opens the door to Pat carrying a straw hat with a pointed top and a chin strap

"Hi! I saw Lennard's truck. Can I speak to him?"

"Sure. He's in the kitchen. Come in and tell me how you are feeling." Kim and Pat walk towards the kitchen. "Good, really good," Pat responds.

To Lennard, Pat says, "The smell is just about gone. Lennard, I won't need the exhaust fan after today. I'll leave it out front."

"Fine, I'll pick it up later."

Kim interjects, "We were just talking about Harry Gellis."

"I'm surprised you let him in your house," Pat quipped.

"What are you talking about? When?" Kim is shocked.

"I saw him walking away from your house Saturday morning. I didn't want to say anything – It's really none of my business and all…" Pat babbles on.

Lennard interrupts her, "Are you sure about that?" He presses the point.

"Sure, I'm sure."

"Brad and I were gone all day! It was the antique center's grand opening. Don't you remember?" Kim begs.

Pat massages her head, "It was such a crazy day for me with the fire and all. But I did see him!" She raises her right hand. "Hand up to God. I'm telling you true." Pat checks her watch as Kim is about to speak.

"Gotta go!" Pat whirled around and headed towards the door.

"But wait!" Kim blurts.

"I can't! I'm cooking Chinese tonight and have to stuff the Wontons. Chin chin," Pat announces as she places the hat on her head and adjusts the strap.

"I'll walk you out," Kim dejectedly accompanies Pat to the door. To Lennard, she suggests, "Lennard, if you have time, please measure the wall for the grab bars."

"I'll do that now." Lennard proceeds to the hallway to measure the wall.

As Pat and Kim walk to the front door, Pat pauses, and in a voice barely above a whisper warns, "You're a nice woman and it is none of my business, but I strongly advise you to stay away from Harry Gellis."

"I'm trying to, Pat. Don't you understand, I have no interest in Harry Gellis!"

"If you say so. Just remember, he plays rough, but I saw him first!"

"Did he hurt you?" Kim says with concern.

Pat rubs her cheek. "Let's just say he has a hair trigger temper and wants_everything his way, every time.

Kim places her arm around Pat and advises. "The first slap is his fault, not yours. But if you stay and empower him, the next slap is your fault." Pat bows her head. "You have no idea what its like to be lonely. Be careful!" Kim assures Pat, "I will."

Pat gives her signature wave and vanishes. Kim locks the door, resets the alarm and returns to Lennard.

"He was in my house! He was at my doctor's office! Last week he lingered outside the bank, followed me into the hair salon, popped up in the supermarket, the cleaners. It is not a coincidence. He knows where I live and follows me around, grinning and making lewd gestures. How do I stop him, Lennard?" Kim cries.

Lennard tries unsuccessfully to calm Kim. "Pat said she saw him walking away. There's no proof he was even in here!"

The telephone rings. Kim grabs it.

Harry sits in his beat-up chair, cigarette dangling, phone nestled between his ear and his shoulder. He plays with Kim's panties.

"Hello!" Kim speaks too loudly.

"Why'd you run out on me? I was gonna buy you lunch."

Kim grabs Lennard and puts the phone to his ear as she mouths, "It's Harry Gellis."

They both listen as Kim speaks, "I don't want you to buy me lunch, call me or talk to me. Is that clear Mr. Gellis?"

"Relax sweetheart," Harry cajoles.

"I'm not your sweetheart!"

"Take it easy. It's just a pet name."

The angrier Kim speaks, the calmer Harry sounds, and the more interested Lennard becomes.

"I'm not your pet!" Kim fires back.

"Shh. I can wait."

"Wait for what? I don't want anything to do with you!" Kim screams.

"Sure, you do. You just gotta get to know me better, that's all. 'See ya' soon Mrs. Kim Wolf." Harry warns and hangs up.

Kim collapses in a chair. Lennard massages his chin and comes to a decision.

"Do you want me to have a talk with him?" Lennard solicits.

"Oh, yes, please! I don't want Brad to know. He is under so much strain."

"Mr. Gellis is obnoxious, I'll grant you that, but he is quite a harmless old man, you know. And if it will make you feel better, I'll have a talk with him after work tonight and tomorrow morning I will put the bars in for you. Okay?"

"Okay," She lamely answers.

"Don't worry. I'll be by about ten o'clock in the morning," he guarantees her.

Feeling a little more secure, Kim becomes more composed.

"Oh, yes. Thank you for everything. I will see you tomorrow. You are the only one who knows what's going on; please keep this between us."

"Of course. Try to relax. 'See you in the morning."

Kim walks Lennard to the door, shuts off the alarm to let him out and resets the alarm.

Kim goes to her office and starts up the computer. She reads several newspapers online and researches wrist watch sites and antique dealers in close proximity to the house. Hours go by and she is feeling fine. She begins to think about Brad and her new plan to heal.

Brad is a willing, supportive partner who denies her nothing. After all, she seems happy, engaged and is becoming vibrant. Her skin is smooth and she's developing a soft natural blush. Her eyes sparkle. Her lifeless hair shines. She is moving more steadily – her balance has improved. How could he not fight alongside this courageous woman? Hope indeed springs eternal and they cling to it with all their might.

Brad returns home that night in a good mood. Brad and Kim kiss and hug a long while.

"Ah, the tighter you hold me, the freer I feel," Brad says with glee. "I had a great day and bought fabulous merchandise. But first, tell me how your appointment with the doctor went. What about your finger?"

"My finger is fine, continue the aspirin, watch my blood pressure and don't get too excited except in the bedroom," Kim announces.

"I'll see to that!" Brad boasts. "By the way, was your new boyfriend on the shuttle?"

"No, he wasn't," Kim says meekly.

"Good! Let me show you what I purchased today." Brad excitedly unwraps several watches.

Kim is impressed and spreads them out carefully. "Omegas!" She proclaims.

"Fabulous, aren't they? All chronographs from the nineteen forties. Tri-colored dials, water resistant type cases," Brad exclaims excitedly.

"I'm so proud of you," she adds.

"Thanks, partner. I need labels. Can you work with me tonight?"

"Sure. I spoke to a friend of the computer guy who can build you a site – a virtual store. He was a NASA scientist. Please consider an on-line business in addition to the antique center."

"I promise, I will think about it. It's a lot to learn."

"Great. I have a trial subscription to a new on-line service that claims to insure total anonymity."

"Who are you hiding from?"

"Spammers."

"What are spammers?"

"People who send junk email. I'm now known as The Muse."

"The Muse? I miss our trips to the library."

"This is so much easier for me. I'm linked to the world and I don't have to leave the house."

"Just don't burn your library card."

"Never!"

"Well, I'm going to change and wash up for dinner." Brad stops to look out the window as dusk settled in. "Isn't this paradise?" He sings.

"I wish." Kim stares out the window as the sky it grows darker. She has much on her mind.

38
Boy's Night Out

It is Randi's turn to host the guys' night out. Randi's territorial house in Fountain Hills is small but neat almost antiseptically clean. Me, Sean and Phil gather around Randi's dining room table and handle recent weapon purchases. Randi checks his watch several times and chews a couple of pieces of gum rapidly; I can't tell if he is concerned or annoyed.

It is time for show and tell. "I picked these up at a police auction. All five armed forces' flags made in the USA." I proudly display my find.

"Nice, Jack," Randi says.

"Sean show 'em your new knife."

Sean removes a dagger from a silver-plated steel scabbard and announces, "Authentic Third Reich you hear me? Like look at that Stag Horn grip." He passes it around for inspection. Look at the markings. Near mint condition."

"Nice Sean," Phil says. "How many does that make it now?"

"Twenty-two," Sean responds proudly. "Watch this." He grabs a piece of paper from his pocket and slices it.

"I wish I could cut Harry Gellis loose from Pima Vista that easy," Randi laments, "we received another complaint.

"The old guy who tried to strangle Phil?" I asked.

"Yeah, that's the one," Randi said.

"What did he do now?"

"Mitzi Benson, the activities director cornered me and complained

145

that Harry Gellis has been doing cannonball dives during the aqua-size class."

"That jerk is going to kill it for all of us, right Randi?" Phil begs.

"All I know is, I spent a lot of time filling out complaint forms because of that bastard. And the community board ignores them."

It seems to me, Harry Gellis is always creating a problem for the boys at Pima Vista.

Randi checks his watch. "I wonder where Lennard is. He's always so prompt." Randi likes Lennard Jayko the construction supervisor at Pima Vista and brought him into the group which doesn't make Sean Mason too happy. Sean is a couple of years older than Lennard and isn't thrilled that Lennard is his supervisor.

"Lennard?" screamed Sean. "You invited Lennard? I work with him all day dude. Do I have to spend personal time with him too?"

"Yeah, I invited him. He's a good guy. So, what of it?"

Sean backed off. "Hey, you do what you want. I'm heading out early for the Mustang. Anyone coming?"

"Nah, I'm going to skip it tonight. I got to get up early, I'm going to the shelter my daughter suggested. I picked out a great little Boxer pup," I announce with some pride trying to hide my excitement, "I named him Lobo."

"So, you gave in and gonna get the dog, huh. Good luck!" Phil confirms. Phil had the evening all figured out. "I'll go with you Sean. Randi, if the wife calls, tell her I went out for cigarettes. I'll call you later."

"I'll wait for Lennard and we'll join you later," Randi said.

The party broke up. Randi checked his watch again. He seemed concerned.

The next morning, I picked up Lobo, a beautiful year old rescued Boxer. Some moron abandoned him on the Freeway six months prior. A good Samaritan took him to the local shelter where he was checked out medically and certified for adoption. I will never understand the cruelty of humans to treat a defenseless puppy in such a horrific manner and will forever be grateful to the good Samaritan who saved him.

I had to go through a long and detailed vetting process to be sure I won't abandon him, have a decent place for him to live and that I am qualified to take proper care of him. I was given strict instructions and a stringent schedule for his care and feeding. I spent a lot of time with Lobo at the shelter before I was able to bring him home.

Lobo is an active puppy which suits me fine. I will take him on all my athletic adventures. My daughter was right, and Lobo is bringing us and the kids closer as a family. Lobo is simply, the best "soul" I ever met and an important part of my life.

39

What Happened to Lennard?

The next morning, Kim rises early, dresses and works on her computer. Brad arranges his watch tools on his desk. They both have a busy day planned. Brad has new clients to see. She is focused on creating a website for him. Lennard is coming by to install more grab bars.

Brad asks, "What are you up to today?"

"I'm working on your website. After I finish on the Net, I will entertain myself with laundry," she chirps.

"Well, I've got new clients to see and I already did my laundry," Brad says with some pride.

"Terrific. Did you fold it and put it away?" she inquires.

"No," Brad admits sheepishly.

"If you are going to do something, can't you finish the job?"

Brad collapses in the chair and stoops over with the weight of the world on shoulders.

"I just can't get it right, can I?" he says dolefully.

"No, it's me. I'm sorry I came off so harshly," Kim confesses.

She massages his neck and kisses him on the head.

"By the way did you see my new panties?" She lightens the conversation.

"The pink ones I gave you?" he asks.

"Yes, I thought maybe they got mixed up with your laundry or..." Her mind seems to wander for a moment.

Brad brightens, "No, but perhaps we can have a date tonight."

"Great idea." Kim is eager to relax with Brad.

"'Looking forward to it. By the way, can you do a search for me on European watches 1920-1960?"

"Sure." For her it is interesting and great fun. She is learning new skills. "I'll have it ready by the time you get home." The mood lifts. They are looking forward to a pleasant evening.

After Brad leaves, Kim frantically searches for her panties; they are nowhere to be found.

She assumes they are mixed up in a drawer or someplace else, so she moves on to the next task. Kim is sure she almost has convinced Brad to have his own website on the Internet; that would be her new focus.

Kim goes back to her office and arranges a meeting later in the week with Amrit Patel the former NASA Scientist just starting out as a web designer.

She refers to the list of healing modalities she reviewed with Dr. Craig and decides to make an appointment with an angel reader, which she anticipates will be fun. She sets that up as well for the following week. Now she waits for Lennard.

Where is Lennard? 10:00 passes. 10:30 passes. Lennard does not show up. "So, unlike him," she thinks. Kim keeps busy. 11:00 passes. 11:30 passes. By noon, Kim is feeling uneasy. She calls the office.

After several rings, Jennifer, the slender tattooed receptionist at the Pima Vista Retirement office finally answers.

"Hi Jennifer. This is Mrs. Wolf on Lot 55. Before I ask to speak to Lennard, I would like you to promise me you will not give out our information to anyone without my permission. Is that clear?"

"I only told Ms. Wilson about you. She insisted on knowing about her new neighbors. I thought that was fair and saw nothing wrong."

"That's not your decision to make," Kim reprimands her.

Jennifer just shrugs and seems dismissive.

"Oh and Mr. Gellis. He said something about picking you up, so you could travel together to the doctor."

Kim is furious. "No one, do you understand, Jennifer? No one. Now, may I speak to Lennard, please?"

"Lennard is in the hospital. He was in a bad accident with his truck last night," she nonchalantly says.

"Oh, no! Is he okay?" Kim begs.

"I don't know," she responds incredulously.

"What hospital is he in?" Kim urges.

"Desert Memorial over on Shea," Jennifer responds.

"Thank you." Kim hangs up quickly and redials.

"This is all my fault," Kim repines.

Kim tries desperately to reach Lennard but is stuck in the automated loop.

"Thank you for calling Desert Memorial Hospital's Quick-Serve Telephone System. If you know your party's extension, enter it now followed by the pound sign. For patient information, press one."

Frantically, she presses one.

"Enter the first three letters of the last name followed by the pound sign."

Frustrated she presses J A Y.

"One moment please. Mrs. Arnett Jaynes is in good condition in maternity and can be reached at Extension 302. For information about another patient, press the star key now."

She jams the star key.

"Mr. Lennard Jayko is in the intensive care unit and is unable to receive calls at this time."

She hangs up and re-dials finding herself in the same loop. She quickly presses zero praying she would reach a human. After several beeps she does.

"Please connect me to the nurse on duty in ICU," Kim is firm in her request.

"ICU. Nurse Radin speaking."

"Can you please tell me Mr. Jayko's condition," she impells.

"Are you family?" Nurse Radin inquires.

"No. I am just a friend," Kim says sadly.

"Then I am sorry, ma'am. You'll have to contact the family," Nurse Radin counsels.

It is that serious. Kim hangs up distraught, remorseful. She is convinced that Harry Gellis has something to do with Lennard's accident and blames herself for getting him involved. She is not of the same mindset as everyone else that Harry Gellis is a just a loud mouthed, harmless old man. She senses danger.

40

Randi Takes Over

Family, friends and neighbors mill around the small but neat territorial home. Mrs. Jayko, 70, wheelchair-bound, huddles with Randi. She clings to a rosary in her hands.

In between sobs she blurts.

"I was there this morning when they took him into the operating room. He was still unconscious. I couldn't even say good-bye to him. Oh, Randi, I feel so helpless. What am I going to do? He was so young. Why? Why? Why?"

"I don't know why. But I do know he's in good hands now. We're all here to help you with anything you need," Randi assures her.

"You're a good friend, Randi. Lennard was very fond of you," Mrs. Jayko says between tears.

"Yes, I'll miss him." Hesitantly, Randi prods, "He didn't show up at my house last night. Do you know where he went?"

"I know he made a stop right after work, then headed to your house. He made another stop at the Mustang to call me. He told me he ran into Phil and Sean," she replies innocently.

"Do you know where he made the first stop?" Randi gently inquires.

"No. Why?"

"His brake line is broken. If he ran over something, I have to know what needs repair around the complex. In the meanwhile, is there anything I can do for you now?"

She pats his hand and in between sobs moans, "Please say a

prayer for my boy.

Out at the crash site, Randi and Christine Lord, the community based police officer inspect the wreck while horses graze in the background. Billy Westin, the tow truck operator hoists the front of the decimated truck.

"Hold it, Billy," Randi orders. Randi scrutinizes the underside of the truck. "Christine, what does this look like to you?"

Christine inspects the underside of the truck. "Broken brake line. He either hit something or somebody whacked it pretty good. Lost fluid, no brakes. I'll have it taken to our impound yard and let the forensic guys go over it."

Randi stands aside. "If there is any indication of foul play, I'd like to know before there's any bad ink."

"I will let you know." Christine continues to make notes while Randi observes her.

"Want a piece of gum?"

"Yeah, sure. Former smoker?"

"Yeah, you too?"

'Stopped a year ago. How about you?

"Six months. "By the way, are you married?" he blurts out.

"No. Are you?" she responds without looking up.

"Never been."

"Interesting. Well, here's my card; take two. Call me."

Back at the Pima Vista Retirement Village office, all is quiet. Randi leans on the counter and directs Jennifer, the receptionist.

"Let me see Lennard's schedule for today."

Jennifer hands him a clipboard. He studies it, chewing thoughtfully.

"As usual he was right up to date," Jennifer contributes with some admiration.

Without looking up, Randi orders, "Please ask Sean to go out to the crash site right away. The fence needs repair."

Jennifer yells towards the back room, "Hey Sean! You gotta get to Pima and Maple to fix something."

From the back room, the response comes back. "I ain't gotta do nothin. That's Indian land. Let them fix it."

Jennifer put her hands up as if to give up.

Randi marches to the back; Sean is startled to see him.

"The crash site borders Pima Vista and it is our responsibility to fix it, so get out there and do the repairs," Randi commands.

"Like I still got ten minutes left on my lunch break!"

"Finish your lunch and go to the site where Lennard had the accident. There are horses that could get loose."

"Friggin' Indians," Sean grumbles.

"By the way, did you see Lennard last night?"

"Yeah, Dude. At the Mustang. He was calling his Mommy. We told him we broke up early, you know? I left after a beer. He was playing darts with Phil who was supposed to call you."

"So, you left before he did?"

"Yeah. So, will I be getting his job?"

"For God sakes, Sean. He isn't in the ground yet." Randi unwraps a piece of gum and walks away disappointed and disgusted.

Randi studies the work orders on the clipboard. "Jennifer, if you need me, I'll be at the Wolfs' home."

41

Randi Speaks to Kim

Randi is in the Wolf's home. He sits in the kitchen with Kim who wears a red sweater over camel colored slacks. She is visibly upset.

"I'll have Sean come by to finish up the grab bars tomorrow. As you can imagine with one man down, we have to rework the schedule until we get more help," Randi informs her.

"I understand," Kim shares, then urgently continues, "Please tell me, Randi, what happened to Lennard?"

Randi took notes and without looking up just answered as a matter of fact, "His brakes failed."

"It's all my fault," Kim whispers.

Randi places his pen down sits up straight and stares directly into Kim's moistening eyes.

"What do you have to do with it?" Randi interrogates.

"Lennard was doing a favor for me," Kim admits.

"What kind of favor?" Randi is intrigued.

"He went to Harry Gellis' house to tell him to leave me alone. The man's been stalking me since I moved in," Kim continues.

"What's that got to do with Lennard's accident?" Randi probes.

"What if it wasn't an accident?" Kim states.

Randi just laughs. "Harry? He's just a harmless old loud mouth from the east."

"Pat Wilson said she saw him coming out of my house while my husband and I were away. I believe her – something personal of mine is missing," Kim protests.

"Why didn't you report the break-in?" Randi challenges.

"She just told me yesterday, but she is so confused about that day her barbecue blew up. I just don't have any proof," Kim explains.

Randi recommends, "Well why don't you and your husband fill out a complaint form."

Kim cut him off. "No! I'll do it. My husband is under too much stress. I don't want him to know anything about it."

Randi isn't convinced Harry is anything more than a nuisance and suggests, "There is a lot of construction around here. Lennard could have hit anything, anywhere at any time."

The wind rattles the screens. Kim jumps at the noise. Randi is cool and comforting but he needs to move on.

"Sandstorm coming. Do you have anything that needs to be brought into the house?"

"No," I'm fine."

Randi hands a frightened Kim his card.

"I'll talk to Gellis. In the meanwhile, call me anytime if he bothers you again."

"I will, thanks."

42

Harry Closes In

Kim prepares dinner. She is uneasy, while checking the weather. The ringing phone startles her.

She quickly answers. "Hello?"

Squat behind a bush in Kim's backyard, Harry, hair blown wild by the wind, clutches a cellular phone.

"Busy house, men coming and going. What's hubby going to say?" Harry quips.

Kim hangs up immediately. The telephone rings again.

"Stop calling me!" she shouts.

"Honey? What's up?" Brad asks sweetly.

Embarrassed, but grateful, Kim responds, "Oh Brad. It's you. I thought it was those damned telemarketers."

"What happened to your manners?" Brad coaxes her, "That doesn't sound like my polite wife. You need to stay calm, honey."

Frustrated, Kim demands, "When are you coming home?"

"I'm delayed at the antique center. I might be…Honey? I can't hear…

Static on the line. The call is disconnected. Kim hangs up. She paces nervously.

Harry, still partially hidden in the backyard, redials his cell phone.

Inside the house, the phone rings. Kim grabs the phone on the first ring.

"Honey?" She calls out.

"That's me, Babe. You should always wear red it brings out your fire."

Kim jumps with fright. She scans the room.

"You're beautiful even when you're upset. I can't wait until we're together."

In a frenzy, Kim limps through the house double locking doors and windows.

"In your dreams, you creep! Why don't you find someone else to pick on?" Kim protests.

The winds pick up. The sky darkens.

"I found what I want, and I always get what I want," Harry states simply.

"I'm not a what. I am a who and you can go to hell!" Kim shouts.

"Stop running around. You'll wear yourself out. I'm sure everything is locked up tight; the way I like it," Harry sneers.

Kim's fear turned to anger.

"I'm warning you! Leave me alone!" Kim threatens.

"Why don't I come in and we can get better acquainted?" Harry teases.

The call is disconnected.

Kim frantically calls the number on Randi's card.

"He's here!" she screams.

"Mrs. Wolf?" Randi asks.

"Harry Gellis!" she blurts out. She is in a panic, grabs for a knife in the kitchen. She checks the alarm. Hobbling from room to room she double-checks the locks on each window.

"In your house?" Randi probes.

"No. On the phone. He can see me!" She is breathless.

Randi is growing impatient.

"Over the phone, Mrs. Wolf? I'm not understanding you," he responds with a chilly calmness.

Exasperated, she concludes, "A cell phone. He's on a cell phone outside looking in."

Interference on the line. The phone goes dead. Kim rechecks the alarm, while clinging to her kitchen knife. The lights flicker. The sandstorm rages. The phone rings. She clutches it and before she could answer, Harry's booming voice taunts.

"Hey, this is fun. But we got disconnected. How about we get connected now."

Static. A series of clicks, a dial tone and the howling wind resonates throughout the house.

The front door unlocks. Kim falls to the floor in a fetal position. She gasps for air and moans as Brad enters the kitchen. Brad runs to her and places her in his arms.

"My God, what happened? Stay put, I'll call an ambulance!"

Kim collapses in Brad's arms. "No, I'm fine. Help me up." They hug for a long time.

"Tell me what happened," Brad is frantic.

He removes the knife from her hands and places it on the counter.

"I just lost my balance. I'm not hurt," Kim soothes.

"Are you sure?" Brad urges.

"I'm sure. I just got frightened. The storm..." she explains.

"Me, too. I guess we're not used to this sort of weather, so I rushed home," Brad points out.

The doorbell rings. Brad situates Kim on a chair and answers the door.

"I'm Randi, Mr. Wolf. We met last week. May I speak to Mrs. Wolf please?"

"Yes, of course. What is this about?"

Randi strains his neck to see Kim hobbling towards them. The back gate bangs. Kim seizes the moment.

"It's the back gate. It won't stay shut. I was concerned it may be damaged slamming in the wind."

Brad shrugs, "My wife takes care of the house."

Kim caresses Brad, "Why don't you get ready for dinner. I'll speak with Randi."

"Okay, if you are up to it," He turns to Randi and adds, "she's had a nasty fall." He checks her cautiously and again asks, "you're

159

sure you're okay?"

"I'm fine now," she reassures him and leads Randi towards the back as Brad exits in the direction of the bedroom.

"Did he try to break in?" Randi asks.

"No, he's tormenting me now. But he will."

"I'll check the alarm system."

With Kim trailing behind, Randi checks the alarm pads, windows and doors.

"This is the best system on the market right now. It would take a professional to get by it."

Grateful, Kim relaxes a bit. "Thanks, Randi. Is there anything else we can do? For extra security?"

"Front and back security doors and extra window guards but I think you are quite safe."

Randi notices the knife on the empty counter.

"I guarantee you he's harmless. Don't let your imagination get the better of you," he chides.

Icily, she insists, I'm not imagining anything! I am sorry to have bothered you."

"I promise you I'll have a talk with Gellis, tonight."

"You'd better be careful."

"Don't you worry about me. If you want to file a complaint, stop by the office at nine o'clock tomorrow morning."

"I will."

Randi exits through the back door. Kim watches Randi through the window as he checks the perimeter. From behind a Bougainvillea bush, he retrieves remnants of cigarette butts which appear to have been stomped on and torn to shreds. "Not enough to test for any DNA," he notes.

43

Kim Takes a Stance

Inside the Pima Vista Village office, Kim sits at a conference table and fills out forms. She checks her watch, fidgets with the contents of her bag and eventually settles down. She glances at the clock on the wall and compares it to her watch. Her eyes dart back and forth from the door to the clock. She's antsy; it's past nine o'clock. She begins to tap her fingers on the table. She reviews the forms for a third time.

Jennifer, indifferent, stamps envelopes and stacks them haphazardly. She offers no solace to Kim. After her stamping chore is complete, she leans back in her chair and twirls her shoulder length hair. They both stare at the clock on the wall.

"Jennifer, remember what we talked about?"

Furrowing her brow, Jennifer answers simply, "Yes, I do."

Kim impels, "Those files are confidential, aren't they?"

Nervous, Jennifer speaks cautiously, "Yes."

"Then have you given out my or my husband's information to anyone except Pat Wilson and Mr. Gellis?"

"No! I told you that on the phone." She pauses, hesitates, "maybe Mitzi Benson."

"It stops here, Jennifer, right now!"

"It will. I swear. Please don't tell Randi. He'll fire me."

Kim mulls it over. "I'll think about it."

They both stare at the clock on the wall. Several minutes pass. Jennifer goes back to twirling her hair. Kim is worried and uncomfortable.

Jennifer speaks up. "'Sorry he's late. It's not like him to keep people waiting. He's a precise kind of guy. When he says nine o'clock a.m., he means nine o'clock a.m. on the dot!"

"Can you call him on his cell?" Kim frets.

"Nope! Only for emergencies – those are the rules."

Suddenly, forty minutes late, Randi bursts through the door. Kim with a sigh of relief, exhales and relaxes.

"'Sorry, I'm late, ladies. There are exposed pipes on the property that need attention. Jennifer, page Sean for me and tell him to get out to Barletta. If he has any questions, pass him through to me, otherwise, hold my calls."

Hastily, Randi gathers some papers and ushers Kim into his office.

"Come in, please."

Sheepishly, she admits, "I was worried about you."

"Me? Lady, I've been through battles written only about in military history books. Believe me, there is no reason to worry about me. Now, have you filled out all the forms?"

Slightly annoyed by Randi's bravado, Kim answers "I have." She hands him a stack of papers.

"Do you really want to take this harassment complaint to the police?" Randi asks as he reviews the documents.

"Yes, I'd like to see that bastard locked up and fined. Harassment is a punishable offense; I did the research."

"Mrs. Wolf, I spoke to Harry Gellis and gave him fair warning. I promise you he'll leave you alone now."

"I doubt it!" she laments.

"Mrs. Wolf, I grant you he is a nuisance but that is all he is, one big pain in my butt. Excuse the language. Frankly with the loss of Lennard, I'm short-handed and a bit on overload so I would appreciate it if we could let this go. I've done all there is to do in this situation," Randi admonishes her.

With a mixture of sadness and embarrassment, Kim retreats. "Let me not waste anymore of your time. I'll go directly to the police."

Kim gathers her things and is about to leave more determined than when she arrived. She knows she isn't going to get any more help from Randi.

"Wait!" Demands Randi. He removes a business card from his desk drawer and hands it to her. Call the teleserve people at the police department. Ask for Christine Lord; she's a friend of mine. She'll work with you."

"Christine Lord? Oh, yes, I met her at Pat Wilson's home the night her barbecue blew up."

"That is correct. She's the community based police officer."

"Thanks, Randi," Kim is truly appreciative. She turns to leave, doubles back and as an after-thought, inquires, "Were you a police officer, Randi?"

Randi relaxes and puffs out his chest as he proudly announces, "Army, M.P. Fort Hamilton, New York. That's how I know about Coney Island."

With furrowed brows and squinty eyes, Kim coerces Randy to continue. "What about Coney Island?"

Nonchalantly, Randi, now distracted by the piles of papers on his desk, remarks, "Gellis mentioned Coney Island once. I think he is from Brooklyn."

Kim absorbs that information like a drowning woman clinging to a raft.

Back home in her office, Kim, speaks over the telephone.

"Yes, Officer Lord, telephone harassment. I know it is punishable by fine and/or prison time."

"That's true, it is a punishable offense but let's not get ahead of ourselves. Do you have substantial proof?"

"What kind of proof do you need?"

"Do you have telephone recordings?

"No."

"Has he sent you threatening letters?"

"No."

"Ma'am do you have any witnesses who are willing to come forward?"

Kim thought about Lennard. She felt dejected and helpless.

"No."

"Ma'am, please understand my position. I need a little more to work with."

"I understand. (pause) I am sorry to have wasted your time."

"You haven't wasted my time. Do you have anything else you can give me?"

"All I have is a record of dates and places where he has appeared uninvited."

"That's a start."

"They are all in public and I guess can be easily interpreted as coincidences."

"Send me your list of dates and places where you feel he has followed you and if you can come up with the kind of proof I described, get it to me as soon as possible."

"I'll do that."

"Good. I'll check him out."

"Please be careful."

"That's sweet, but I am a trained police officer. I'll handle it."

Feeling a bit better about reporting her concerns to the police, Kim relaxes on the couch and watches a television rerun. Her mind is running a hundred miles an hour. She doesn't pay much attention to the naïve young talk show host interviewing a man in disguise hidden behind a screen whose voice has been altered.

The host concluded, "So then you are saying there is a strict code of silence in your world, am I right?"

"You betcha! *Ratatatat, know what I mean?*" laughs the guest.

"What happens if someone breaks that code?" The host asks innocently.

"He ends up as part of some landfill or at the bottom of a river." The man mumbles his answer.

"The host presses on. So, terms like 'cement shoes' and 'sleeping with the fishes' are true?"

The man laughs now as does the audience. "Yes, little boy. It happens. You can read about it every day in the New York Post."

Kim turned off the television and exits to her office. She starts her computer, waits for the dial tone and dials up her computer. She waits patiently for a connection and her screen to come to life.

"*Ratatatat?* Where have I heard that before?" Kim searches the Internet for Crime Families. She finds information for victims of crimes. Her search for The Mob yields nothing. When she enters Mafia, names, hierarchies and rap sheets of alleged Mafioso appear.

Under Brooklyn, she finds the same. Kim researches the <u>New York Post</u> and reads the first headline. '<u>Chimp</u> Bites Man in Caboose at Rail Yards.' Stifling laughter, she reminds herself, "I remember that! Oh, how I miss those headlines!"

44

Boys Night Out and Christine

I know Christine Lord slightly, but she'd have no reason to share information with me. I am out of the loop and basically around the station to coordinate volunteers.

Me, Randi, Sean and Phil are at the Mustang bar, the place we frequent the most. It's a quiet night, no games on the television, just a few stragglers in addition to us regulars. Randi takes me aside and asks me to join him at a table in the back of the bar where it is private and dark. Before we have a chance to speak, a tall red-headed voluptuous woman dressed in tight jeans and a yellow top that emphasizes a healthy chest, small waist and hips that could launch a battle ship, slithers into the booth and plants a long deep kiss on Randi's lips. Randi's whole demeanor relaxes.

I sit quietly, embarrassed and curious at the same time. I have never seen Randi in any situation other than ram rod straight, hair perfectly combed, clothes crisp and clean and in control. After that kiss, he is like a bowl of jello and…well, just plain silly, giggling like a little girl. Randi is in love with a beautiful gal who could have been a Las Vegas showgirl, just my type.

"Jack, say hello to Christine Lord, my fiancée."

"Wow, congratulations. I had no idea. You're with Teleserve, right?"

"Right."

She reaches into Randi's pocket and takes out a piece of gum

166

and begins to chew as rapidly as Randi. I guessed she too, is a former smoker.

I had seen her around the station but only sitting behind a desk, no makeup, hair pulled back. Sean and Phil end their dart game quickly and join us. Randi introduces them, orders a round of beers and we all toast the happy couple. Eventually, Sean and Phil resume their dart game and Randi, Christine and I talk about police work in general, their budding relationship and how they met. I watch as Sean and Phil fight over a dart game and I am getting bored.

Quietly, Randi carefully removes a plastic bag from his pocket and hands it to Christine.

By the look on Christine's face, I know exactly what she is thinking. I didn't like friends asking me for favors when I was on the force. Just before I retired, Sean once asked me to run a license plate for the address of a pretty girl he saw parked on the street. You can't do that. So, I am a little put off and wonder what Christine will do.

Christine confronts Randi. "What do you want me to do with this?"

Oh, oh, that doesn't sound good. I'm thinking perhaps I should leave them alone and start to get up to join Sean and Phil at the dart board.

Randi grabs my arm. "No, it's alright stay." He turns his attention to Christine and explains,

"Last night I went over to talk to Harry Gellis about another complaint from one of the residents and got a partial print on my badge."

"Why?" Christine and I ask in unison.

"Lennard talked to Gellis before the accident and Gellis bragged about how he took care of him. I just want to cover all the bases in case Lennard's death wasn't an accident."

"Tell me what happened," Christine urges Randi.

"You gotta hear this. So, I rang the doorbell. The jerk came to the door in his underwear." So I said, "Maybe you can put on a robe. I need to talk to you, Mr. Gellis."

"Now what!"

"The winds are picking up. Mind if I come in?"

"I ain't receiving any company."

"We can do it out here."

Harry unlocked the security door and let me into the doorway.

"There ain't nothin' to do. First Geronimo, now you. Whaddya want?"

"You wouldn't know anything about Lennard's accident, would you?"

"What did he do? Fall off his Tommyhawk?" Harry joked.

"He was killed in a traffic accident."

Harry shrugged, "It's news to me." Harry yawned.

Harry's indifference infuriated me

"Let's get to the business at hand. I'm still receiving complaints from women residents about your less than gentlemanly behavior."

"Get lost!" Harry dismissed me.

"I'm tired of filling out stacks of forms about you. This time, I'll see you go before the board; not your so-called representative, Mr. Grimm," I threatened.

"We'll see about that!" Harry poked at my name badge with his fore finger.

"Screw you and your little tin badge. You ain't no cop!"

"You've been warned, Mr. Gellis," I reminded him.

Harry slammed the door in anger.

I entered my truck. From the glove compartment I removed a plastic bag and carefully placed my badge in it, hoping you would check it out. Randi continued and assured us, "If I find out he had anything to do with Lennard's accident, you may have to hold me back."

"Whoa! I'll take care of it," Christine agrees.

She marks the plastic bag and places it in her pocketbook.

Sean approaches the table with a round of beers for us. I think he overheard us talking about Gellis. He placed the beers on the table. We thanked him.

"Drink up guys. You're playin' the winner."

Sean returned to the dartboard, threw a dart and hit the bullseye!

"Take that, you big ox!"

45

Was Lennard's Death an Accident?

A couple of weeks later, we had another boy's night out and Christine showed up again.

Same scenario. Me, Randi and Christine sit at a table in the back. Sean and Phil fight over a dart game. We talked about Lennard and his accident. Randi told me and Christine quietly what happened when he went out to the site of the accident after he told Sean to fix the fence.

"The winds were fierce as I parked next to Sean's Chevy truck. I arrived just as Sean was loading tools into the back of his truck."

"Do you need any help?" I asked him.

"Nah dude. All done. Like, it was a small job."

I examined the site, patted Sean on the back and said, "Thanks, Sean. It looks good."

Sean secured his tools in the back of the truck and pouted, "Still don't see why I had to do it."

Exasperated I added, "Because you are the best man for the job. 'Meet you back at the office."

"Yes, chief." Sean said sarcastically.

I had enough. He's a friend and all but I am still his boss. He provoked me. I confronted him.

"Why did you hate Lennard so much?"

"The special treatment he got. You think he was better than me?" Sean raised his voice.

I had to remind him, "Lennard worked his way through college.

170

You won't even get your GED."

Sean held up both hands, "My hands are my degree. You know I can fix anything, anytime with any tool you throw at me."

I agreed, "Buddy, I know your skills and I respect them but that's not enough if you want a position of responsibility. You gotta stop complaining and learn how to work with people, all people."

Sean hung his head. "Yeah, yeah, I'll work on it. Can I go now?"

"Not yet! The cops are looking at the brakes on the truck Lennard was driving. Am I in for any surprises?" I asked.

"Whoa, dude. Like I don't know nothin' about it. I swear." Sean backed away, hands up.

I warned him, "You'd better be straight with me."

"Yeah, well, maybe he got just what he deserved," Sean said as he entered his truck.

"Watch your mouth!" I was so angry. I almost punched him.

A couple of weeks later, Randi, Christine, Lobo and I are out at the shooting range. Sounds of gunfire and beating drums rattled in the background; Lobo is used to it. He accompanies me everywhere and is a great companion. He's an active, social pup and loves being part of anything and everything I do. We're attached at the hip.

Targets dot the desert landscape. Randi takes a shooting stance. Christine and I wait to the side. Randi hits the bullseye.

We high five him. He asks Christine, "What did you find out?" She responds, "We lifted two good prints from the brake line; they're not Sean's." We are all relieved.

"What about Gellis?" Randi pressures Christine.

"Nothing, yet. It's taking longer than usual to get the information." Randi just shakes his head in disgust. "I swear if these guys had to organize a firing squad, they'd do it in a circle." We all laughed at that and left the firing range.

46

Sedona, Arizona Where God Plants His Lips

Sedona located in the upper part of the Sonoran Desert in Northern Arizona is simply exquisite. With its spectacular views, magnificent sunsets and splendid skies, photos, at least Kim's photos, cannot capture its natural beauty.

Known for its unusual naturally sculptured red rocks, a thick layer of red to orange colored sandstone found only in the Sedona area and energy vortexes, it attracts artists, spiritual healers, photographers and film makers who have created vibrant communities in the 19.2 square miles that make up the total area.

Visiting Sedona is an experience one does not forget. The ride is easy, the views majestic.

The weather is perfect as Brad and Kim stroll through the famous village and enjoy the stunning views. They admire the assorted antiques and art displayed by the various artisans in white tents. There is an area filled with culinary treats and the center stage offers music and dance. They are having fun.

Poli Mana approaches. "Hello, I am so glad you could come. Let me show you around."

Brad is mesmerized. "I have never experienced such a pleasant feeling of calm within. It's like I am floating instead of walking. I feel so light."

Kim is thrilled. "This must be where God plants his lips."

Poli Mana reminds them, "We are in the vortex. Come to the healing circle with me. We end with the sweat lodge."

Brad is incredulous. "A sweat lodge in the desert? I pass."

Poli Mana patiently explains, "It's a spiritual cleansing to promote balance and self-realization."

Brad is eager to get to the antiques. "Kim, why don't you go. I will pick you up at five o'clock."

Kim is elated. She's been eager to experience the first of many alternative methods of healing she has been researching.

Poli Mana takes Kim's arm and guides her the short distance to the backyard of her home. The desert landscaping is set in circular patterns. The sweat lodge is in the center. Lounge chairs and hammocks surround the lodge. A diverse group of people mill around quietly

Poli Mana asks Kim gently, "Why do I sense you are deeply troubled?"

Kim exhales and responds," I can handle Brad and myself, but a third person is trying to interfere in our lives."

"Oh, yes, the big man with white bushy hair," Poli Mana states.

Kim is shocked, "How could you possibly know?"

"When I meditate on you, I see him and feel his energy. It is chaotic."

Kim is agitated but relieved to be able to talk about it with someone who understands.

Anxiously, she cries, "He's stalking me. I reported him to the police, but I haven't told Brad."

"Each situation presents an opportunity for growth. Perhaps this reflects some old unresolved issue."

That goes way beyond Kim's understanding of how the universe works.

"Oh, I don't know. We need to settle in."

Poli Mana suggests, "Maybe you can confront him in person."

"I've tried! He wants to hurt me, and I don't know how to protect myself!"

Poli Mana places her arm around Kim and stays absolutely still for a moment, eyes closed. Kim doesn't move. Then Poli Mana looks at her turquoise encased Omega watch.

She announces, "It's time for the healing circle. Come, get your power back."

Gregory, a muscular, elderly Native American dressed in traditional garb wafts cedar and sweetgrass smoke on Kim as she stands fascinated, eyes wide absorbing the energy of the environment.

Poli Mana leads Kim to a group seated in a circle holding hands. She is graciously accepted and joins hands with strangers on either side of her.

Poli Mana and Gregory sit in front of the group eyes closed. Poli Mana speaks softly.

"Place your hands in your laps and close the first three fingers of each hand. Close your eyes and relax. Breathe deeply, rhythmically. If it helps, inhale through your nose to the count of four and exhale through your mouth to the count of six to start."

Poli Mana checks each person in the group and continues, "Let's bring the earth's power into our bodies through our energy centers, gates and transformers along the spine and up into the head. Relax."

Kim is fussy. She's uncomfortable, anxious and not quite understanding what Poli Mana is talking about. She tries to relax; begins to count her breaths.

Poli Mana touches her shoulder gently.

Several minutes pass.

"Focus on your energy and relax. As we embrace the power of the earth, the mountains, the sun, moon and stars of the sky let us send healing to the world, its hungry, homeless, sick, sad and troubled. Let us imagine abundance and love for all and especially for ourselves. Relax."

Kim relaxes, smiles eyes closed.

After Poli Mana is sure everyone is relaxed, she invites all in the healing circle to enter the Sweat Lodge, a dome shaped structure made from tree limbs and twigs and covered with a canvas.

47

Gun Fire and Drumbeats

The sound of gunfire melts into the rhythmic sounds of Gregory beating drums in the sweat lodge. It is a large tent.

In the center is an earthen dug pit filled with hot rocks. Poli Mana enters, sits in front of the hot rocks and motions for Kim to sit next to her. As people enter and sit around the hot rocks, Gregory brings in additional rocks, blesses them with sweet grass and cedar and douses them with water to create hot steam.

"Stay as long as you wish. If you must leave, do so," Poli Mana advises soothingly. She is the only one who speaks. "Adjust your body for relaxation. Lie down or sit. There are no requirements other than your comfort."

"Focus on your breath. Release the toxins of your mind, body and spirit. Breathe."

After a few minutes, Poli Mana adds, "Feel free to offer silent or spoken prayers. No one interrupts, and no one reveals what is said. Relax."

An old man faintly sings. Three people gingerly mutter. Kim cries softly.

Awhile later, in Poli Mana's backyard, Kim rests. Poli Mana hovers. People mill around, speak in soft tones.

Kim sighs, "I feel so relaxed."

Poli Mana smiles and reminds her, "Excellent! But remember, you've just begun the process of ridding your body of toxins.

Cleansing and repairing, renewing and revitalizing tired muscles, bones and tissue takes time and patience. I suggest you rest for a couple of days, meditate at least twice a day and wear red socks."

"Red socks?"

"I'm told by other healers, that red socks will help you stay grounded. Your illness, Kim. What have doctors told you?"

"That there is no cure," she says simply.

"This is a wonderful time to develop your spirituality and creativity." Kim seems to dismiss that thought. "I'm overwhelmed right now. How do I thank you for today? Surely you must charge a fee for the lodge."

"I usually do, but not you." Poli Mana reaches for a package under the chair and gives it to Kim.

Kim opens it and clings to it with tears streaming down her face, exclaiming, "A Kachina doll! Butterfly Girl?"

"Yes." Poli Mana smiles. "May it help you on life's path and lead you to the good things in life. May you move like a butterfly."

"She's precious," Kim sighs.

"Yes. Gregory carved it for you."

"When?" Kim inquires.

"Right after we met," Poli Mana answers.

"Why?" Kim is puzzled.

"Gregory is my father. He believes we were related in a past life. Does that surprise you?"

"Yes. But I am so calm inside right now, I am open to anything."

Brad drives up and waves from the car. "Hi ladies."

Kim kisses him and exclaims, "Brad, I feel wonderful."

Sadly, Brad counters. "At least one of us had a good time. 'Sorry, we have to leave so early Peggy, but we've got to go."

Kim and Poli Mana embrace. "Thank you for a lovely day. I hope to see you soon." Kim says.

"You will. Don't forget the red socks." Poli Mana waves.

As Kim enters the car, she caresses the Kachina doll and adds,

"Please thank Gregory for me."

"What is that?" Brad prompts.

"A Kachina doll. I'll explain later."

Brad drives away quietly. "Please pull over," Kim urges.

Brad always on alert, seems worried. "Are you okay?"

"I'm fine. I want you to spend a few moments looking at this gorgeous scenery. "

Brad resists, "We have a long ride home."

"You're missing this beauty. You can't work all the time. Take Alfred Hitchock's advice to a nervous actress 'true chopper'."

"I have no idea what you are talking about. Can we go now?"

First tell me another word for true.

Exasperated, Brad blurts "I don't know – real?"

Correct. Now what's another word for chopper.

Brad takes a deep breath. He knows if he doesn't play the game, they will be stuck there for a long time. "How about ax?'

"Correct! Now put the two words together."

"Realax? Very cute, relax. What happened to you today?"

"I don't really understand it myself, but I feel calmer inside. Maybe that will make me stronger outside. I think I may be getting better."

They hugged, wept in each other's arms and stared at the beauty of Sedona before heading home. She clung to the Kachina doll all the way home.

48

Kim and Brad Return from Sedona

Kim and Brad enter the house, happily exhausted. Well, Kim is happy. Brad is disappointed that he didn't find enough merchandise to justify the long trip in his mind. Kim feels renewed. They cuddle on the couch, while Kim admires her Kachina doll.

"Beautiful place but another disappointing day for business," Brad laments.

"We need to concentrate on an advertising campaign," Kim announces.

"You mean like local papers?"

"No. Specific editions of some publications, flyers and post cards to reach your target audience," she explains.

"Sounds expensive."

"Not if we know what the competition is doing. It's an investment and we can't waste our advertising dollar. We'll evaluate the CPM."

"You sound like a Madison Avenue type. I can't keep up with you. Now what are you reading?"

"I looked up marketing strategies on the Internet, then I called one of my friends from work. Her husband who is in advertising and marketing explained it to me. CPM is cost per thousand. I can do it all on the computer!"

Brad laughs and says, "I'm glad you are on my team!"

Kim responds, "Honey, I am your biggest fan." She pecks him on the cheek and announces, "I'm going to play a little."

Off she goes to the office. Kim places the Kachina doll on top of her computer. She connects to the Internet.

As she surfs the Net, she says to herself; "Let's start two years back." The New York Post site pops up. She scans the front page headlines. February 20th catches her attention: 'Brooklyn Mob Boss DeBola Indicted.' "I remember this."

Just as she is about to read the article, Brad enters. "Hey night owl. It's past our bedtime." She makes a note to revisit the site and read the article.

Kim dutifully shuts down the computer and takes Brad's arm.

"C'mon Princess. Let's make like newlyweds," Brad winks and sweeps her off her feet.

"Oh, do I appreciate this. My legs stopped talking to me hours ago. I'm so fragile," she says somewhat embarrassed.

"Most beautiful and delicate things are," Brad says in between heavy breaths as he struggles to balance her in his arms.

"I'm concerned about your back," Kim reveals.

"Maybe you can cut down a bit on the Haagen Dazs," Brad proclaims.

49
Trouble in Paradise

The next morning, Kim sits up in bed, a heating pad draped over her legs which rests on a wedge; her arms in braces.

"Brad, would you mind taking my clothes out of the dryer and bring me my red socks?"

Flitting around the room, preparing for work, Brad inquires, "Aren't you getting up?"

"No," she responds.

"Then why do you need your red socks?" Brad asks.

"Why do you ask?" Kim retorts.

"Well, I just wondered why you need your socks if you're not getting dressed. Are you cold?" Brad challenges.

"No, I'm not cold. You know, if you're going to do your laundry, why can't you do mine at the same time? Are you afraid my panties will peek at your jockey shorts?"

"No, but..." Brad tries to explain.

Kim is impatient and angry. "And if you are going to make yourself breakfast, can't you put some gruel into a bowl for me?"

At his wits end, Brad confronts Kim. "You know, I just don't understand you. One day you want to do everything. The next day it's all on me. How am I supposed to know what's when?" he complains.

"Ask!" Kim shoots back.

"You're so secretive."

Kim relents, "I try not to bother you."

Frustrated, Brad weakens. He sits at the edge of the bed. "Then how am I supposed to know anything? I'm trying, but I just keep screwing up. I want things back like they were."

Defiantly, Kim states, "They're not going back. It takes me two hours to do what I did in twenty minutes. How the hell do you think I feel?"

"I no longer know how you feel. All I know is I can't shake the feeling that someday I'm going to wake up and you won't and that gives me night terrors. I stay up most nights just listening to you breathe," Brad hollers.

Kim takes his hands in hers. "I understand, and I am afraid of losing you as well. In fact, that is all I am afraid of. Eventually, we'll both die. But do you want your last memory to be of us fighting?"

"No," he admits.

"Then stop living in denial and mourn when I'm dead. I need help! If you can't do it, I need someone who can," Kim insists.

Brad suddenly leaves the bedroom and returns shortly after with the Yellow Pages in hand. He places it on the bed.

"What is this supposed to mean?" Kim is stymied.

"You can look up a maid service," Brad announces.

"Can't you do it?"

"No! I'm trying to get my business going and I can't handle this right now."

"I see." Kim is disappointed.

Brad gathers his keys, change and sunglasses. "I'm going to work. I can't stand this. One day you're sick, one day you're not. I don't know who you are anymore! Brad exits and slams the door.

Kim looks around the room. She is hurting, badly.

"Terrific. Just when I need you the most, you take off. I'll do It myself! I don't need you. I don't need anybody."

She hurls the telephone book across the room and knocks a vase off the dresser.

"Great!" She gets out of the bed and cleans up the mess.

Two hours later, she calls Brad. "I'm sorry. I'll do better, I promise. Come home early, I am preparing a nice steak dinner. "

50
Treadmills and Angels

Kim realizes she needs help. As Dr. Craig recommended, she calls Sally to make arrangements for physical therapy at the local hospital. Brad is supportive and rearranges his schedule to attend with her three times per week. She works with two physical therapists who design a program geared to her needs. It is slow going at first. When she begins, she is unable to stand on the treadmill more than a minute and a half. Over time, she will increase her speed and time dramatically.

The rules are strict. No patient is allowed to work on a machine unless a therapist is present. Kim and Brad arrive one day for their appointment – no therapist is present, but the music is playing. So, they dance. Well, Brad dances, Kim puts her feet on his and holds on. The therapist arrives and waits until the song is over.

"I wish my wife looked at me like that," he sadly comments. He then suggests they take advantage of a new program which includes nutritional therapy, art therapy and music therapy which they do.

In between appointments with the nutritionist, art therapist and music therapist, Kim continues her research about the human body and is amazed to discover the complexity of the body which has 206 bones, 640 muscles and many organs, the skin being the largest.

Over time, she studies the various body systems such as cardiovascular, digestive immunological, skeletal, circulatory and respiratory, etc.

Referring to her list, she finds an angel reader in the downtown area and makes an appointment for her and Brad. If Brad does not believe in it, he says nothing.

Ms. Florence, the angel reader, welcomes them warmly. She operates out of a small commercial space in a building with a dozen units. Ms. Florence is about fifty, heavy; she wears loose clothing, colorful and flowy; a long skirt and oversized top. She perspires as she flits from corner to corner of the small dimly lit office and prepares her reading table. As she brings a deck of cards, a cloth, water, a candle, etc., to the table, she rambles on about her troubled daughter. Kim and Brad both wonder why she can't use her healing powers to help her own daughter and why she isn't better prepared for their arrival. They've given her no information except their first names.

She finally asks them to sit around the table while she recites a silent prayer over the cards. Neither Brad, nor Kim can see what is on the cards. She hands Kim the cards and instructs her to touch each card gently. She closes her eyes as Kim gently touches each card as directed. Florence is awestruck, opens her eyes quickly and declares "I never saw this before! You two share the same angel! I'll read you as a couple. Oh, isn't this fun!"

It was and as Ms. Florence explained, angels surround Kim and Brad on their journey and according to her it will be a long and successful one. She warns about a relative who is drinking too much, which turns out to be true and gives them satisfying facts about relatives who passed but came forward to deliver messages of hope and comfort. It was an interesting afternoon.

51

Harry and Mr. Grimm Part Company

Harry and Mr. Grimm sit at the far end of the stands during the ladies' barrel racing event at the Arizona state rodeo.

Announcer: "Next up, Lou Ann Clark, the pretty little lady from Tucson up on Butterball. She won the last…"

Harry focuses on Lou Ann. "I'd like to saddle up with that one," he sneers.

Mr. Grimm commands, "Pay attention! This time it's gone to the police—telephone harassment."

Harry is clearly not interested. "So, what? They'll take away my telephone?"

"Besides a fine, you could serve jail time." Exasperated, Mr. Grimm asks, "Tell me genius, how did they get your fingerprint?"

Disbelieving, Harry responds, "Whaddya talking about?"

"The PD sent in a print of your right index finger. They're checking for priors. We are not amused."

Harry is nervous. "But still, you got that covered, right?"

"Yes!"

"So, tell me, big-shot. It's against the law to call a dame?" Harry blusters.

"It is the way you do it."

Harry's attention is on Lou Ann Clark as she finishes her race. The audience applauds.

Announcer: "Let's hear it again for the pretty lady from Tucson." Wolf whistles, shouts and applause fill the arena.

Harry leans over to Mr. Grimm and quips. "Hey, I'm just a friendly old guy looking for love. No one's going to blame me for that. What's your point?"

Mr. Grimm firmly speaks. "My point is this; we've gotten you out of hot water for the last time."

Harry confronts Mr. Grimm, "Yeah? What does that mean?"

"It means, Harry, that if I don't have your word here and now, that you will never contact this Kim Wolf woman again, we separate you from the program."

Harry holds up his middle finger and shouts, "Screw you and your crummy witness protection program!"

Harry storms out of the arena. Mr. Grimm remains seated and punches numbers into his cell phone. "Banion/Gellis is terminated from the program. I'll give you a full report tomorrow."

52

Not Even A Parking Ticket

Me, Randi, Sean and Phil are at the Mustang Bar. Randi and I are at the pool table, chalking our cue sticks. Phil and Sean are close by at the dart board. No matter how often they play, neither one of them is very good at it.

In walks Christine. She is becoming a regular at our 'Boys Night Out' and Sean and Phil aren't happy about it. I have mixed feelings. She is a nice gal, but she's changed the energy of the group and change is not easy for some folks. Phil and Sean hardly speak to her. Besides the weather, she and I could always talk about police procedure.

She greets us all, kisses Randi passionately and joins me and Randi at the pool table. She's a pretty good player. Sean and Phil go back to their dart board, disgusted looks on their smirky faces. Jealous? I think we all are.

"Randi the report came back on your boy, Gellis." She informs him.

"And?" Randi queries.

"Clean, not even a parking ticket," she says nonchalantly.

Sean strains to hear her.

Randi continues. "Gellis is such a pest. I'm getting awfully tired of his shenanigans."

Sean grabs Phil by the arm. "Did you hear that? We've got to get a message to Harry Gellis. You hear me?"

"What are you talking about?" Phil seems anxious.

Sean continues. "That jerk's threatening our jobs. That's all I got, man."

Phil mulls that over and responds, "I don't want to get into any trouble."

"I promise you – we won't get into any trouble."

"So what do you think we should do?"

Sean took Phil in the corner. "You and me. We organize a little covert action and teach him a lesson."

53

Ladies Day Out

Kim and Poli Mana stroll past the Native American Indian displays at the Heard Museum.

Sadly, Kim reports, "Brad's business is not doing well."

"And you?" Poli Mana inquires.

"I worry about Brad and frankly, the pain is getting worse."

"Brad's business will improve with time. On the other side of your struggle is great triumph. You're building strength and with that comes power."

"I can't see what you do. I feel as if I am losing my energy."

"You need to get involved with your creativity."

"My creativity will have to wait. We need to focus on Brad's business."

"Perhaps you are being creative with his business," Poli Mana muses.

Kim laughs. "Yes, perhaps I am – on the World Wide Web."

"And the big man?" Poli Mana inquires.

"Ah, yes. Harry Gellis. He scares me," Kim admits.

With eyes closed, Poli Mana cautions, "Don't let him wear you down. He doesn't understand that where there is love, there is no need for control. I recommend imaging. Surround him with white light, explain your feelings, then send him healing."

Kim dismisses the advice and proclaims, "I'm not you."

Poli Mana touches her lightly on the shoulder and encourages her. "You can do it. When I meditate on you, I see you soaring in silence.

"I'm at a loss here."

Trust yourself more. I'll send you and Brad healing. Try to meditate twice a day, upon wakening and just before bed time."

Kim agreed, "I will."

Poli Mana is satisfied. "Good! Get some rest and wear your red socks."

Kim smiles, hikes up her prairie style skirt and shows Poli Mana her red socks. "I've got them on."

54

Raw Emotions

Later that day, Kim rests on the couch and watches television. She focuses on a talk show about sexual harassment. She hasn't learned anything new. She turns off the television, puts the first three fingers of each hand together, rubs her red socked feet together and closes her eyes.

A ringing phone awakens her.

"Hello?" she answers.

"Hi. I need to work late tonight. Can you hold dinner for me?" Brad asks. His voice cracks, he sounds sad.

"Sure," Kim says, "are you alright?"

"No, not really." Brad sighs.

"Come home and we'll talk it all out."

"I can't now. Just know that I love you so much." Brad hangs up the phone, puts it to his heart and whispers, "Please don't die on me babe; you're all I got."

Kim goes to the bedroom to lie down. She closes her eyes.

Agitated, she popped her eyes open. Harry stands over her, shirtless, trying to undo her blouse. She screams.

Her scream startles her awake. She removes the dream catcher from the dresser and hangs it on the headboard remembering Lennard's words, "It catches the bad dreams and allows the good ones through."

"Some image." She says to herself.

Kim is up and awake. She proceeds to her office, turns on the computer and waits patiently for the dial up connection.

She reads aloud as she revisits the two year old February 20th article 'Brooklyn Mob Boss DeBola Indicted.' It was the lead story with a photograph of Joseph DeBola. Handcuffed, he was led out of the courthouse under guard.

"Joseph 'Joey the Gyp' DeBola is led from federal court after his indictment for the murder of his brother in a Mob power play."

She scans the article and continues; "Giaccomo 'Sugar Jack' Angiotti of Angiotti Candies and Angelo Narlino, a butcher, both of Brooklyn have also been indicted. Key witness Rosa DeBola, daughter of the victim turned state's evidence. She was arrested for money laundering"…"Oh, this is juicy," Kim continues.

She scrolls forward. The story contains another photo. "Her testimony was backed up by her husband, a Mafia soldier with convictions for burglary, manslaughter and rape."

Kim reads on and excitedly turns to the photo of Rosa and her husband on the courthouse steps and continues to read the caption: "Mafia Princess Rosa DeBola and hubby Johnny 'Honest John the burglar Banion.'"

"Wait a minute!" Kim exclaims. "Let me maximize this photo. Oh, my God!"

Kim discovers that Harry Gellis is John Banion. She grabs her Kachina doll and pets it as she paces around her desk. She replaces the Kachina doll and tries to relax, taking a meditative posture, breathing deeply.

She is unable to relax. She continues to pace; her mind racing a mile a minute. "Smart, very smart. Safe and sound at Pima Vista Retirement Village? Maybe not so safe."

Kim scrolls back and makes notes of the names of the men arrested. She picks up the phone and dials.

"Operator. How may I help you?" a firm voice answers.

"Operator, I need two numbers in Brooklyn, please," Kim says authoritatively.

The operator responds, "The first one, please."

Kim reads from her notes. "Angiotti Candies, two T's."

A slight pause, the operator says.

"718 555-8727. The second one, please."

Kim again refers to her notes. "Narlino's Butcher Shop."

After a moment, the operator discloses, "718 555-2751. Will that be all?"

"Yes, thank you." She hangs up the phone.

From her drawer she removes Harry's Gellis' King of Hearts card and places it by her computer.

She dials the phone.

A female voice answers. "Angiotti Candies."

Kim, a little nervous inquires. "Hello. Do you have an email address so that I may send a purchase order?"

The female voice seems annoyed. "Ya' want candy, ya' tell me what you want. We deliver. You pay in cash. Got it?"

"Got it. I'll tell my boss." Kim responds and quickly hangs up.

Kim is on a mission. She dials another number.

"Meats! How may I help you?" The female voice asks.

Kim repeats her request. "Hello. Do you have an email address for purchase orders?"

"Narlino@cobweb.com," is the response.

"Thank you." Kim hangs up. She creates an email and inserts Harry Gellis' information.

"Cobweb, it should be Mobweb," she mutters to herself. She stares at her email and in a crisis of consciousness removes her hands from the keyboard as if they are scorched. "I must be crazy. I can't send this." She minimizes the email, sets the Kachina on top of her monitor and paces around the office. "What is the right thing to do? Clearly, Harry is hiding from his old friends. How can I use this information to protect myself?" I really can't. Deep in thought, she leaves the computer open in email mode and goes to the kitchen to prepare dinner.

55

Harry Puts His Plan in Motion.

Harry's at home, dressed in black. He dials the telephone. Harry holds a handkerchief over the mouthpiece and fakes an accent. "Mr. Wolf? A friend of mine gave me your card and I have a watch to sell. Are you interested?"

"Sure. What have you got?" Brad is elated.

"One just like the picture on your business card."

"Are you sure it's the same

"Sure, I'm sure."

Can you tell me anything about the watch over the phone?"

"I don't know nothin' about watches. It belonged to my older brother."

"Are the hands on the watch identical to the ones on the card?"

"Yeah, yeah, yeah, same."

"Is the name on the dial the same?"

"Yeah, yeah, yeah, the same."

"How much are you asking for your watch?"

"I don't know. You figure it out."

"I've got to see if first for a cash offer. Do you have a receipt for the watch, instruction booklets or the original box?"

"Nah, nah, nothing like that. Listen, I'll bring it over to the antique center. How long will you be there?"

"I'll be here until 8:00 I'm in booth 11."

"Good. The name is Johnson. Wait for me now. Bye."

A storm is brewing. Dark clouds form.

Harry dials the phone.

"This is Mr. Gellis confirming my charter to Mexico. Are you sure we'll get out in this weather?" He pauses and waits for the answer. "Yeah, yeah, all cash. Send the car early. I want to get goin'."

Within minutes, Carl calls The Boss. "Boss. Good news. You were right, the poker game paid off. The guys think his name is Harry. Willie treated him very carefully, told them he was a dangerous guy. He fits John Banion's description. Gino just called me to tell me a guy named Harry Gellis booked a private plane for Mexico tonight!

"I'm gonna pick him up in a couple of hours.

"Great work, Carl. If it is him, I want you to leave the phone open so I can hear his last breadth."

"On it, Boss. Then can I come home? It's awfully hot here."

"When I know John Banion is dead."

56

Christine Speaks to Harry on Kim's Behalf

Harry, dressed in black, packs jewelry and documents into his suitcase. He wraps a pistol in a shirt and stuffs it under the documents. He puts a ski mask in his pocket along with Kim's panties.

Harry methodically and quickly moves through his house, checks all the rooms, picks up small items he needs for his trip plus cash from the freezer. "Cold, hard cash; nothing like it. Thanks, Willie!" He discards the wrappers and fills his money belt with the cash, In the bathroom he retrieves a waterproof package from the toilet tank. More cash. "This ought to tide me over. Huh, I like that. Tide me over. Huh, Tidy Bowl." He discards those wrappers and crams the money into the pockets of a black suit which hangs on the door and the money belt he packed in the suitcase.

Harry roams through the house one more time, examining drawers, closets and cabinets. He places his bulging suitcase by the door. He takes one last look around and salutes. He checks his watch. "This won't take long. I'll be back within the hour."

Just as Harry is about to leave, Christine rings the bell.

He's pressed for time. He opens the door.

"Yeah whaddya want?"

Harry is annoyed until he sees Christine. Harry's roving eyes ogle every inch of her body.

Christine shows him her credentials. "I'm Christine Lord, the community based officer. Can we get out of the wind sir?"

Harry opens the door wider and they both step into the hallway.

"Zowee, wowee. Is it my birthday? Come in, you gorgeous hunk of woman."

"Sir, I'm investigating a charge of telephone harassment."

He crossed his wrists and said, "Baby, take me now. I'm yours."

"I'm not here to arrest you and I suggest you not call me baby."

"Alright, alright, just don't ignore me."

"Sir, I need you to focus."

Harry's mood changes from playful to irritated.

"Now what's this about a phone call?" Harry feigns innocence.

"A telephone harassment charge has been filed against you by Mrs. Kim Wolf. I am here to record your side of the story."

Harry reprises his innocent charm act and spread his arms to explain. "It's simple, I saw her around, thought she was cute and called her a few times. You can't blame me for trying. Got it? I got needs."

Christine is firm. "Mrs. Wolf is apparently not interested in your needs. I am directing you to cease all contact with her."

"Gimme a break, will ya?" Harry is disgusted.

"Do we have an understanding?" Christine demands.

"Sure, sure, anything you say, officer. Cross my heart and hope to die." Harry crosses his heart and puts his hand up to God.

"Excellent. I will contact Mrs. Wolf and see if she will agree to drop the charge." Christine is pleased.

"You do that." Harry checks his watch and ushers her out the door.

57
The Attack

Kim looks out the window at the darkening skies. Nervous, irritable and in pain, she seeks an immediate remedy. Haagen Dazs Vanilla Swiss Almond ice cream. She curls into the couch, red socks on, ice cream in hand. Lost in thought, she continues to savor the ice cream. When the container is half empty, she smoothes it out and puts it away. She attempts to meditate. That doesn't work.

The telephone rings. She jumps, answers and relaxes. It is Brad.

"Hi, honey," she coos.

"Hi, love. There's a storm brewing; I'm on my way home."

"I'm glad you are coming home early."

"I was supposed to meet someone about a watch, but Peggy offered to take care of it for me."

"Thank her for me."

"I will. Why don't I bring home dinner and we can just relax tonight. Maybe watch an old movie?"

"Sounds perfect. I will take a shower and be fresh as a daisy by the time you get home. Love you."

"Love you, too. Can't wait. Gotta go."

Kim relaxes, goes to the bedroom, positions her robe on the bed. She places her cane outside the door to the bathroom.

Harry puts a ski mask over his face, peeks through the bedroom window and watches as Kim prepares for her shower.

"Oh, nice. Take it off, baby."

In the living room, the lights on the alarm panel go out.

In the bathroom, the shower runs. Kim enters the bathroom and closes the door.

Harry enters the house through the back door; it squeaks open. He stands quietly for a moment.

"Good, she didn't hear me." Harry creeps across the floor.

Brad waits in a long line at a fast food restaurant while a new cashier is being trained.

Harry lurks outside the bathroom. Through a crack in the door and with the help of the tilted mirror he gleefully watches Kim on the bath chair rinsing herself off with the shower head extension. He moves her cane.

Brad strains to see the road through the swirling winds of the sandstorm. Traffic is slowed.

Kim completes her shower, wraps herself in her robe and reaches for her cane. It is gone. She laboriously moves down the hall. Harry follows behind her.

"Brad?" she calls out.

"Try again," Harry sneers.

"You? How did you get in here?"

"Tricks of the trade. Just crossed some wires in the control box."

"Take off that stupid mask and get out of here, right now!"

"Not yet, sister. I've waited a long time for this."

He leans toward her and sniffs.

"Mmm, you smell good."

Harry takes out her panties and brushes them across her neck. She grabs for them. He teases her and pulls them back. They drop to the floor.

Brad is stalled in traffic. He munches on a chicken leg.

"Get away from me. Brad will be home any minute," Kim threatens. She is as angry as she is frightened.

"Brad's been delayed. He's waiting for me to show him a watch."

"If you hurt him, I will kill you," she warns.

Harry laughs, looks down at his pants and grabbed his bulging crotch.

Kim tries to retreat to the bedroom. Harry grabs her by the shoulders and spins her around. He cuts her off.

"Hey, don't limp away."

She grabs the handrails for support. She lashes out with her leg and kicks him behind the knee. He loses his balance and stumbles.

She's terrified. "Brad, Brad, where are you?"

She hobbles towards the living room, spots her cane at the end of the hall and holding herself up by the handrail reaches it just as Harry recovers and comes after her. She fends him off and moves towards the den. He grabs for her she throws the cane at him and hits him squarely in the chest which startles and momentarily delays him.

She lunges for the phone. Harry grabs her hand puts it behind her back and pulls at her robe with his other hand. He attempts to kiss her neck.

"You're disgusting!" she cries. She struggles to break free while he attempts to unzip his pants.

"Stand still!" he commands.

"Get out of here, now you pig."

"Right here, baby, right now. You've been driving me nuts from the first time I saw you."

She kicks, slaps and pokes him as he attempts to grope her.

The guy is a beast, feels nothing.

"Stop moving, you'll like it."

He pushes her up against the desk. Her computer is on and connected. She continues flailing her arms to no avail. He slaps her face.

"Help, somebody please help me. You filthy, miserable bastard."

"Yeah, talk dirty to me."

Harry has Kim pinned against the desk. He again attempts to kiss her. The Kachina doll falls onto her face preventing him from touching her. He grabs the Kachina doll and slams it onto the computer. The screen is open and in email mode. The computer beeps. An audio message announces, "Your email has been sent," which distracts them both.

Kim calls out," DeBola, Narlino, Angiotti, dirty enough?"

"What did you say?" Harry is stunned.

"You just committed suicide Harry Gellis or should I say John Banion?"

Harry glares at the screen, sees his photo. Harry is thoroughly confused and furious. He screams.

"What does this mean? Tell me right now, what does this mean."

"E-mail, honest John, e-mail. You just sent your Brooklyn buddies an email."

"What!"

"They know who you are and where you are."

The attack is over. Harry zips up his pants, Kim rearranges her robe. Harry turns swifty towards her and slaps her face. "I ought to kill you right now."

"Will that make you feel like a real man?"

"How did you…?"

"You are an unprotected witness now. Run John Banion, Run! I'll give you a head start."

"That's nice of you, bitch. "They can't touch me. Besides, by the time they get here, I'll be sipping Margaritas on the beach."

He grabs his ski mask and sprints out the back door."

She falls to the floor and laughs and cries at the same time.

A bunch of tough guys sit around a store front office with a sign above it which reads Narlino Meats. The Boss sits behind his large heavy dark mahogany desk with his newest open computer, sipping a double expresso.

The Boss concentrates on the screen. The computer beeps and an audio message states, "You've got mail."

Kim's email is received by The Boss. He opens it.

"Holy, shit! We hit the jackpot! Look at this!" The guys gather around. "So, John Banion is living as Harry Gellis at 19301 Quaking Aspen Drive. Write that down."

The Boss dials his phone. "Carl, your hunch is correct. Harry Gellis is John Banion - stay on the line, I'm forwarding an email to you." In his excitement The Boss spills his double shot espresso on the keyboard.

"Shit. The keyboard is fried. Joey, go to the basement and get me another computer. A fresh one while I talk to Carl. Carl, got Johnny Boy's or should I say Harry Gellis' address?"

"19301 Quaking Aspen Drive. I'm on it."

Get over there and take care of him right now!"

"Who sent you the email, Boss?"

"Again, with the questions. How the hell do I know? The keyboard's shot."

Kim pulls herself together, locks the door behind Harry and tries to reset the alarm. Remembering what Harry said, she goes outside, unclips the jumper wires from the open box and buries them in the trash. She closes the box, quickly goes inside and resets the alarm and the pressure pad.

She goes to the bathroom, puts cold water on her face and weeps. "Brad where are you?"

Brad puts daisies on the seat next to him and drives away from the supermarket parking lot.

Kim dresses hurriedly, puts on makeup to mask the redness from Harry's slaps and goes to the den. She straightens the room, finds her panties and buries them in the garbage. She unplugs the computer and places the Kachina doll back on the monitor. She dials the telephone.

"Hello, this is TheMuse. I'd like to close out my account immediately as of this minute."

The young man at the other end of the phone responded. "Okay, let me call up your account. (pause) We can extend your email trial another ten days if you like."

"No. Cancel it right away...I'll hold."

After an endlessly long two minutes, the young man returns to the line. "Okay. I deleted it. You're officially canceled."

"Thank you more than you'll ever know. Good-bye."

Lightening, strikes. The lights flicker on and off. Howling wind and thunder cover the sound of the garage door opening.

Brad playfully sneaks into the house with his flowers and food containers.

Kim and Brad meet unexpectantly in the darkened hall. "Get away from me!" Kim screams. She pummels Brad. The flowers and food containers scatter.

"Honey, please. It's me. I'm so sorry, I was playing."

"Where have you been. I needed you!"

Brad holds her close. She melts in his arms and quietly regains her composure.

"I wanted to surprise you. I bought dinner and desert. See? I even found daisies. You said you'd be fresh as a daisy."

"Oh, Brad what have I done to your beautiful flowers?"

"That's okay. I'll get them." Dejected, Brad gathers the flowers and the food containers. Fortunately, they were all sealed.

"Let me help you. We'll put them in water." Kim takes the flowers from Brad's jam packed hands.

Brad arranges the food containers on the counter. Kim primps the flowers in a vase. They do not make eye contact.

Brad put a smile on his face.

"I brought chicken legs. Some of them are missing though." At a poor attempt to be funny he remarks. "Someone must have broken in and stolen them."

"Oh, Brad." Kim cries.

Brad holds her close and examines her face. The makeup does not cover the bruises.

"What happened to your face?"

"I slipped getting out of the shower and fell against the door, face first."

"I'll get some ice, but first let me kiss it and make it better." He held her face gently in his hands and brush kisses her.

"I'm glad you stood that guy up." Kim hugs him with every bit of strength in her body.

Brad tends to her bruise and nonchalantly remarks, "He sounded like a phony anyway."

Kim ices her bruise while nestled in Brad's arms.

"I'm so sorry I wasn't home when you needed me. But I was kind of wanting to celebrate."

"What are we celebrating?"

"I sold more today than I have this past month."

"Then we should celebrate."

"Three people asked me about the classy cards you did on the computer and I know the flyers brought in a lot of people. Thanks, sweetie."

"I'll do anything to help you. I love you so much, more than you will ever figure out."

They kiss. Kim winces. They tender kiss.

Brad says, "You know, I've been thinking. I should have my own web page."

"Wonderful! And you should have your own domain name as well."

"I have no idea what that means but can you take care of that that for me?"

"Anything you need."

Brad picks Kim up and dances with her in his arms.

"Tell me, how hot does it get in that sweat lodge?" He asks.

"Oh, you'll go back to Sedona with me?"

"I'll arrange it with Poli Mana."

They kiss passionately.

Brad sighs, "This really is paradise."

"Oh, yes. Yes, it is."

58

Harry Goes for a Ride

Harry literally runs home. Perspiring heavily, he changes his clothes and puts on the suit hanging by the door, stuffed with cash. He checks his watch and paces by the door. He organizes his suitcase, puts on his money belt and makes a phone call.

"Yeah, Gellis. Are you sure we will get out in this weather?"

The voice on the other end is encouraging, "Not to worry, sir. The car is on its way."

Carl calls The Boss. "I'm on the way to get Harry Gellis. I'll make sure he misses his flight."

A town car pulls up to Harry's house and parks next to the Neighborhood Crime Watch sign. Nervous, Harry checks the time, picks up his suitcase and with a small salute, bids farewell to Pima Vista Retirement Village leaving the door slightly ajar.

Outside of Harry's house, Carl exits the town car and opens the rear door. He's wearing his dark sunglasses, a dark blazer over black slacks, a forced smile and a bulge in his pocket. Harry hesitates.

"Good evening, sir."

"Yeah, yeah."

"I'll take that for you." Harry reluctantly gives Carl his suitcase. Carl opens the trunk and places the suitcase next to a shovel inside while Harry stands aside the opened back door. Carl slams the trunk closed and grins at Harry.

Harry slowly slides into the back seat. He has a feeling something isn't right. "Yeah, yeah, Let's get goin'."

Carl enters the car.

"Where to, sir?" Carl asks with a wide grin.

"What are you, an idiot? Didn't your boss send you to pick me up for the chartered plane?"

"We're early. I thought maybe you wanted to stop somewhere."

"Don't think." My old boss used to say. 'You'll weaken the team.' Just drive me straight to the private airport."

Carl laughed at that, and answered, "Yes, Sir!" Things couldn't have been any easier for him.

"I'll just call it in. Carl reaches across the front seat for his IBM Smart Phone. He pushes several buttons and reports simply, "I have Mr. Gellis with me now."

Harry's uneasy. "That was a lot of buttons you pushed. Isn't your boss local?"

"It's a new phone. You have to put in a code first, see?" Carl holds up the phone for Harry to see."

Harry relaxes and sits back. "Computers, phones. The world has gone crazy with this new technology shit."

"I agree, sir." Carl makes a sudden move. He jumps out of the car and yanks the back door open. Before Harry can react, Carl presses the barrel of a nine millimeter Glock into his face, "Hello Johnny."

Harry tries to resist. Carl spins him around and strikes a blow from behind. Harry collapses, sprawls across the back seat. Carl hops back into the car and drives to a desolated area near the private airport. He parks, calls the boss.

"I'm waiting for the sleeping beauty to wake up."

"Maybe you hit him too hard."

"Nah, he's movin' around."

"Alright, don't make it a saga."

Harry regains consciousness. He's disoriented, weak.

Carl stands guard, gun in hand, aimed directly at Harry. Carl puts the phone on the hood of the car. He opens the passenger door.

"Get out of the car, Johnny or should I call you Harry?"

Harry stumbles out of the car. He looks around. He sees small planes in the distance.

"Listen, I got money. Let me go to Mexico and you'll never hear from me again. I swear."

"On the ground, Harry." Carl kicks Harry hard in the stomach.

Harry winces in pain. "Gimme a break."

Carl kicks him again. Harry rolls in pain and spits. "Fuck you."

"Feel the pain, Harry. You caused a great deal of pain to a lot of people you piece of shit."

"C'mon, you don't have to do this." Harry whines.

"On your knees, Harry. Take it like a man."

Harry attempts to crawl away. "POW!" One shot to the back of the skull. It is all over.

Carl picks up his phone.

"So, Boss, you heard?"

"You did good. Now go through his pockets and his suitcase, keep whatever you find but bring me any papers he was carrying. Then I want you to give him a nice burial – someplace with a view.

"Then what?"

"Then I want you to get rid of this phone. I'll get you a new one."

"When can I come home?"

"As soon as you are done."

Carl digs a shallow grave and dumps Harry's body into it after relieving Harry of his watch, money, wallet and keys. Carl reviews the contents of Harry's suitcase, pockets the additional cash, gun and papers he recovered from Willie's apartment.

Carl stomps on the phone and buries it in a different area.

59

Sean and Phil Execute Their Plan

As the town car disappeared down the street, it passed Sean's truck coming the opposite way. Sean parks a little way from Harry's house.

Sean and Phil dressed commando style get out of the truck.

An agitated, sweaty Phil asks. "Do you think this is a good idea?"

A confident Sean replies, "The storm is perfect cover. Besides which we're just gonna scare him a little."

They skulk outside of Harry's house, looking in the front windows. The wind picks up; sand and tumbleweed blow by them.

Sean notices the front door is ajar and suggests, "Let's go in."

Phil retreats. "I don't know, Sean. Maybe this isn't such a good idea."

"You want to lose your job over this old creep?"

"No, but..."

"Keep quiet and follow me."

Christine Lord, the community police officer patrols the area. Over her radio a female dispatcher calls, "A287."

Christine answers, "A287 go ahead."

"Respond to possible 457 in progress at 19301 Quaking Aspen Drive."

Christine drives to the site. "Gellis again? A297 ETA four minutes. Call Randi Loughman at Pima Vista and ask him to meet me."

Randi and Christine drive up in separate cars. Christine silently signals to Randi to look at the door. The door to Harry's house is wide open. Hand on her gun, Christine moves toward the open door ahead of Randi. She stops short. She hears rustling and whispers in the bushes. Christine withdraws her gun." Police! Come out of there with your hands up."

Sean and Phil came out from behind the bushes; hands above their heads. "Don't shoot. It's us."

Randi throws up his hands, thoroughly incensed. "Oh great." He removes two fresh pieces of gum from his pocket and chews dynamically. He automatically hands a piece to Christine.

Christine, plainly amused, asks, "What are you guys doing here dressed like that?"

Phil answers, "We only wanted to scare Gellis."

"Yeah." Sean agreed. "We figured if we shook him up a little, he wouldn't cause any more trouble. You hear me? Isn't that what you wanted, Randi?"

Phil added. "We looked in and the place is a mess. He's gone, man. We didn't do nothing wrong. I swear."

Christine takes out her notebook and begins writing. Without looking up, she says simply. "You're trespassing."

Phil teeters on the edge of hysteria. "You're not going to arrest us, are you?"

Randi and Christine exchange knowing looks but say nothing.

Sean jumps in, "We were just going to scare him. You hear me?"

Phil continues, "We just wanted to help. "

Randi takes command. "Do you mind if I handle this internally?" he asks Christine.

"No, but I still have to fill out a report. I got the call."

Randi glares at Sean and Phil. "Okay, you, two, back to the office and wait for me."

Randi and Christine watch as Sean and Phil get in Sean's truck and drive away.

"How do you want me to handle the report?" Christine presses Randi.

"How about as Pima Vista employees they responded to suspicious circumstances and somebody thought they were breaking in?"

"Sounds good to me. You take care of them." Christine concurs.

"Thanks, sweet face. What about Gellis?"

"Let's check it out."

Randi and Christine cautiously enter Harry's house.

"It's the police, Mr. Gellis. Are you alright, sir? Mr. Gellis?"

They separate.

KITCHEN: Christine explores the kitchen. The freezer door is opened. She shouts to Randi. "He's not here." She picks up bank wrappers from the floor, places them in a baggie and puts it in her pocket.

BATHROOM: Randi examines the bathroom and notes the toilet tank cover is in the sink and more bank wrappers are on the floor.

"What a mess."

"Pick up some of those wrappers, Randi. I have a hunch they may be connected to another case."

BEDROOM: They meet in the bedroom. The drawers are open and cold weather clothes are strewn about. Christine picks up girlie magazines from the floor and notices a box of panties.

"Horny bastard. Souvenirs?"

"'Sure looks like it." Randi agrees.

They move into the living room and Randi finds the missing tripper from the pool filter. He exclaims, "That son of a bitch. He's the one who screwed up the pool and almost killed Mitzi Benson."

Next to the tripper, is a knob. Christine picks it up, holds it to her flash light and shows it to Randi.

"Do you think this is the gas knob off Wilson's barbecue?"

"Could be. What do we do now?"

"First we have to find him. I have to lock up the place and do some paperwork. Let's talk later." Christine bags the tripper and the knob.

Back at the Pima Vista Office, Randi is distressed; Phil is jittery and paces nervously.

"I told you it was a stupid idea, Sean."

"No, you didn't; you wanted the excitement. Don't lay this all on me, Phil."

"Well, it was your idea."

"Yep and it is still a good one. I'm just sorry that creep wasn't home."

They freeze as Randi enters.

"What the hell were you guys thinking? Sean you are stupid #1 and Phil, you're #2."

Phil's dripping sweat and feverishly wiping his glasses.

Sean speaks up with conviction, "Really, Randi, I didn't think it was that big a deal."

"That's right. You didn't think. Would Lennard have done anything like this?"

"Mr. Perfect," Sean whispers under his breath.

"That's right, Sean. Mr. Perfect." Randi tosses an envelope to Sean. Sean catches it.

"Mr. Perfect left that for you the night before he died."

Sean opens the envelope. He targets a $50.00 bill.

"Read the note, Sean," Randi insists.

"From Mr. and Mrs. Wolf. You deserve this for all the work you did." "Like this will come in handy," Sean says and quickly jams the money in his pocket.

"You bet it will. You're both suspended for a week without pay. It'll give you time to think about what jerks you've been."

60
All is Well

Brad prepares breakfast for two. Kim reclines on the couch, ice on her face. The television is on.

NEWSWOMAN:

Damage estimates from last night's storm are high. Most power outages have been restored and cleanup efforts continue. Today's forecast after this.

Brad turns down the volume.

"I found a lady to clean and she'll stay with you when you are having a flare-up. She doubles as an aide if needed. How did I do?"

Kim kisses Brad. "When you are clear, no one can touch you. I appreciate your doing that. It will be a real help to me."

"I guess I've been more scared about the future and what might happen, when I should be living in the present and enjoying every day."

"I'll do a better job of monitoring my energy and try not to overdo things. When I don't feel well, I'll just tell you and we'll work it out from there."

"That makes sense."

"Then we won't be arguing so much. I can't stand that."

"Me neither. Please forgive me."

"Forgiven and please forgive me, too."

Brad kisses Kim's hand.

Randi drives around the development. He comes upon an exposed irrigation pipe. He examines it closely. "Brake fluid."

The doorbell rings. Brad answers. "Hello, Randi. Come in. Can I get you some coffee?"

"No thanks, I had breakfast."

"Honey, we have company. Randi is here."

Brad leads him to the living room. Kim turns off the television.

"What is this about?"

Randi asks, "Have either of you seen or heard from Harry Gellis within the past twenty-four hours?"

Brad responds, "No. Why do you ask?"

Randi states, "He seems to have disappeared. We're canvassing the neighborhood."

Brad responds, "Huh Is that so? Do you think he wandered off – dementia?"

The doorbell rings. "It's like Grand Central around here. I'll get it." Brad says good naturedly.

As Brad leaves the room, Randi observes Kim's face.

"That's a nasty bruise you have there."

"I slipped in the shower,"

Brad returns with Pat.

Brad adds. "She has a balance problem. Please excuse me but I have to get ready for work. Kim, you'll be okay?"

"I'm fine. Go ahead." Brad lingers for a moment.

Pat looks at Kim's face. "I saw your truck, Randi. Anything wrong?"

"We're asking anyone who knows Harry Gellis if they've seen him in the past twenty-four hours."

"I certainly didn't see him." Pat haughtily announces. She peers closely at Kim. "Who punched you in the face?"

Brad repeats. "She fell in the shower. She's fine. Now if you will excuse me folks. I really have to get ready for work." Brad hurriedly heads towards the bedroom.

Kim turns to Pat. "Mr. Gellis seems to have disappeared."

"Hooray!" Pat quips.

"Maybe he went on a trip. He told me he wanted to go to Mexico." Kim suggested.

"That's right! He complained all the time about being bored. But he told me once he'd take me with him. Well, the heck with him and good riddance!" Pat huffs.

Randi replies, "This is serious ma'am. We have reason to believe he was involved in the explosion at your place."

"Oh, my God." Pat is upset.

"Now, again! Have you seen or heard from him recently?"

"Oh, no. No. I haven't."

Randi turns to leave. "We'll figure it out. Don't you ladies worry now."

Kim offers, "Pat, you can stay here with us, if you are concerned."

"That would be nice. I'll make dinner."

"Fine."

"I'll make my famous Chicken Kiev."

"I'll prepare dessert. Randi, you are welcome to stop by," Kim adds.

"I'll think about it."

Pat heads towards the front door. "I'd better be going. Das Vedanya, everybody."

Pat practically skips out the door.

Randi approaches Kim and stares at her bruise. "Anything you need to tell me?"

"Yes. Have a seat."

Randy sits next to her, looks around for privacy, leans in and says, "Tell me."

"Thank you." Kim says simply.

"Thank you?" Randi repeats.

"Yes, thank you. I think your little talk with Mr. Gellis helped. He hasn't bothered me since."

"Good. I also want to put your mind at rest about Lennard's death. It <u>was</u> an accident. He ran over an exposed pipe over on Grassy

Spring, lost his brake fluid and eventually lost control of his truck.

According to eyewitness statements and later investigators, it was dark as Lennard drove his truck down a lightly traveled road. Oil leaked onto the pavement. He applied his brakes; they failed. He sped through a red light into an intersection. Traffic was heavy. He turned the wheel sharply to avoid an oncoming vehicle. Propelled off the road, he crashed through a fence into a tree. Slumped over the wheel, he was rendered unconscious. Blood spewed from his head. It was called in immediately and an ambulance was on site within minutes, but they just couldn't save him. We lost a good man."

"I lost a good friend. I appreciate your sharing that with me. I'll walk you out." Randy rises to leave.

61
What Happened to Harry Gellis?

Christine is now regularly joining us at the Mustang. Soon after Harry Gellis disappeared, it was boy's night out and Christine. As always, Phil and Sean are at the dart board fighting about who actually won the game; Randi, me and Christine are huddled over beers discussing her experience with Harry Gellis.

"You'll appreciate this, Jack. I was investigating a harassment complaint against Harry Gellis and went to check him out. It was the same night he disappeared."

She turned to Randi and apologetically stated, "Sorry, Randi but he was much nicer to me than he was to you. I rang the bell and he grumbled behind the door until he opened it and saw me. I observed he acted like he had an appointment and was in a hurry. He took note as the winds picked up and seemed anxious about the weather."

"What do you think happened?" I asked.

Randi reported, "Mrs. Wolf and Miss Wilson think he took a trip to Mexico."

"Mrs. Wolf?" I repeated.

Christine added. "She's the one who filed the harassment complaint."

I had no idea Harry Gellis was giving Kim trouble.

All I remember is that John Banion as Harry Gellis, was often the topic of conversation amongst my friends who worked at Pima Vista Retirement Village.

A few months later bones and a skull were found in an abandoned part of the small private airport. It was a professional hit; one shot to the back of the head at close range blew off his nose and rearranged what features were left. Small hole, big blast, probably a hollow point bullet. Maybe a nine-millimeter. Clean, no evidence, no witnesses and dead bodies left in the desert heat for months don't talk.

The forensic guys had a puzzle on their hands. Saliva, hair, blood, fingertips gone thanks to the animals and the elements. Eventually they were able to extract DNA from the bones and he was identified as another relocated witness named John Banion, living by the name of Harry Gellis. The investigators were frustrated. There were dozens of guys who wanted Banion dead; he and his wife put several people in prison back in New York and there was a big bounty on his head.

Then he was gone. The shooter was never found.

Resources were stretched thin. After all leads had been thoroughly investigated, no new information was gained, and that case remains open but inactive.

62

The Reunion 2009

I ran into two old buddies of mine, Matt and Jeff, also retired from the force. They worked on two open cases from back in 1994; the murders of two guys in the witness program. They tell me there is new evidence in the John Banion/Harry Gellis case. I'm eager to learn what it's all about.

I am about to go to a twenty-fifth anniversary reunion of volunteers and Kim will be there. I contacted her when I saw her name on the list of attendees and offered to pick her up and drive her home. She was happy to hear from me. We were friends and worked well together. That was back in 1994; it's 2009 and I wonder what she looks like fifteen years later.

I admit I always had a thing for her which is unusual for me. Being over 6'3" I never dated anyone under 5'7" and I liked them long and lean. If circumstances were different, I would have liked to pursue more than our friendship.

What I remember about Kim is that she was quite literal and took life very seriously. She never talked about her past nor speculated about her future. She's always exuded a fresh intelligence and a wry sense of humor, yet she had a quiet disposition and was totally focused on the moment.

She kept secrets well but shared and celebrated all of life's pleasures. If anyone had a birthday, engagement or anniversary, she either baked something or gathered everyone for a lunch out plus dessert. She was a good listener and didn't judge.

Unfortunately for me she was, and I gather still is in love with her husband Brad. When I called, she sounded happy and content. Contentment, I often wonder what that must feel like. I'm restless. My timing has always been off in my personal life. I have never seemed to be at the right place at the right time.

I loved often and had a lot of sex but there's never been a woman I cared about who was also a friend. Someone I just wanted to spend time hanging out with just talking or going to a movie. Respect, that's what it is. I respect Kim. I never crossed the boundary of our friendship and still live in hope. I know it's foolish and always felt like a sloppy teen around her but she's the only woman I met who came close to the whole package.

My palms are sweaty. I'm about to pick her up.

I'd know her anywhere. Kim looks well and happy. Instead of blond hair, her hair is sparkly white and pleasing to me she's managed to keep her figure. She still wears her thin wired-framed glasses, no longer walks with a cane and but limps slightly.

Her husband Brad is as gracious as ever. They are a wonderful, loving couple and the romantic glow between them seems to have outlasted the ravages of normal aging. It has been a long while since we've seen each other.

It should be an interesting evening.

We are comfortable with each other and pick up our conversation as if we spoke just yesterday

"Kim, you look wonderful. How have you been?" I ask.

"Fine just fine. Brad and I are busy and happy." She responds.

I love the lilt of her voice soft and calming. We catch up on old acquaintances those who passed and those we hope to see at the party. The ride to the venue is short.

The hotel is elegant a resort actually, with a stunning view of Camelback Mountain. The food is plentiful and displayed on long tables throughout the ballroom. Kim and I stay together during the many speeches which thankfully are brief, humorous and filled with good cheer. When the speeches are over, we each go our own way and stay busy with old friends for a while until Matt and Jeff, two of the guys I'm sitting with, bring up the tattoo case she helped solve.

Matt and Jeff were partners in the Violent Crime Division. They are both six feet tall, have brown eyes, same brown haircuts and have similar builds; long torsos, muscular arms and legs. They worked out together, spent vacations with each other and despite the fact that they are both retired they still seem inseparable. If one were to believe the rumors although they are both married with six children and eleven grandchildren between them, one might think they were more than partners.

Matt and Jeff introduce me to Peter, a newbie to the department with a smirk a river wide who I personally want to smack and wipe that grin into yesterday. I'm told he's a rising star in the department, tough, smart and educated. He is an arrogant little prick, who will make it to chief I am sure. Peter is interested in our old cases, so Matt, Jeff and I fill him in.

We discuss a case in which Kim helped. We call Kim over to the table and ask her to tell us how she knew we missed a vital clue. As she sits, I notice her grimace. She's in pain and I think to myself I'd better get her home but once she relates the story, the pain seems to subside, and she appears to be fine. I remember how she suffered in silence and never complained. For her it was always about the work.

"I don't know how we missed it," I lament.

"Because it was a newly formed gang and by their own admission the behavior among the gang members was to pay homage to their fallen friends by tattooing the names of the dead on different parts of their bodies. First it was the arms, the forearms, the shoulders, then the legs and the calves. If it were a best friend, it was near the heart. Good friends got the neck, but the names of all fallen gang members were honored somewhere on the body.

If you remember I was the one responsible for entering the photos into the arrest records of the gang members, so I had an opportunity to study the tattooed names. There was one particular gang member who was conspicuous.

The other gang members looked up to him because he supposedly had so many friends who died. He manipulated them into believing he was some important hero. All he did was use his twisted philosophy for power. He became their leader and led these poor stupid kids into believing they were helping their community."

Peter stifles a yawn; I accidentally kick him under the table.

Kim caught it and with a hint of a Mona Lisa smile leaned in and added. "You see, it made no sense to me that a man with a swastika tattooed across his chest would tattoo a Jewish name on his neck as a place of honor reserved for good friends unless he was bragging. Besides he was the only one in the gang with the tattoo of a swastika."

Peter bolted upright. She had his attention now.

Peter asked. "How did you know it was Jewish name?"

Kim replied. "The name on his neck was the same as my mother's maiden name."

"We felt pretty stupid missing it. His arrest record included several crimes against minority persons and properties. Once Kim checked him out, she brought her findings to me and I had someone investigate him further," I added.

Kim reassured me, "It wasn't a common Jewish name, so you wouldn't have known. Besides, we didn't miss it. We caught on to his sick little game. The tattooed name was a victim, not a fallen friend. And as it turned out so were other names spread across his chubby shapeless body."

Peter questioned Kim. "That would be quite arrogant, don't you think?"

Kim advised, "So is killing someone over a cultural difference. It's called *racism*."

We remained silent while she removed her iPhone from her pocketbook and began to type. "I want to get this right." She read from her iPhone. "As defined in Random House Webster's College

Dictionary, racism is a belief or doctrine that inherent differences among the various human races determine cultural or individual achievement, usually involving the idea that one's own race is superior. It's basically hatred or intolerance of another race or races."

She waited for a response. We were all thinking about what she said.

Peter queried, "So, what is the meaning of *prejudice*?"

Kim referred to her iPhone and read, "Prejudice is an unfavorable opinion or feeling formed beforehand or without knowledge, thought or reason. Any preconceived opinion or feeling either favorable or unfavorable. Unreasonable feelings, opinions or attributes expressed of a hostile nature regarding a racial, religious or national group."

Peter was relentless. "What's the difference?"

Kim responded quickly. "Here's an example. There is a famous black actor who says in Hollywood he faces prejudice every day, not racism but prejudice simply because of the color of his skin."

Lesson over. The interrogation began.

Peter: "What year was that?"

Kim, "1994."

"Did you enjoy your work?"

"I thoroughly enjoyed my work at the department." She smiled broadly at me, Matt and Jeff and continued, "especially the luncheons when we had spirited debates about current events which often included the latest crimes."

Matt and Jeff just nod, grunt and agree. They add nothing to the conversation but stay and listen.

I jumped in as memories flooded back. "We often got together with a group of civilian workers and volunteers and discussed the current crimes at lunch. The O.J. Simpson case inspired heated conversations, right Jeff?"

"Right! They were fun!"

"No one at the lunch table thought he was an innocent man," adds Matt.

"There was plenty of discussion about the baseball bat attack on Olympic figure skater Nancy Kerrigan," Jeff contributes.

"We all suspected a competitor," Kim shares. We're all engaged now as memories flood back.

"But the one that elicited plenty of laughter was the Paula Jones civil lawsuit for sexual harassment against President Clinton while he was governor of Arkansas," Kim reminded us.

"I knew there would be other lawsuits. It was a hoot." I was having the best time.

Kim was visibly disappointed. Not at me, I hoped.

She sighed and said, "As good a president as Clinton was, he just couldn't keep it in his pants. I never understood why it all went public. It was a huge embarrassment and I believe lowered the standards of the office of the President of the United States."

Peter asked, "Why shouldn't the public know?"

Kim seemed impatient. "Because it is none of our business what anyone does in the privacy of his or her home. His cheating is his wife's problem. He had a daughter to consider–too many people were hurt by the scandal especially children and we took our eyes off what was really important."

"What is important to you?" Peter challenged.

"National security, a healthy economy, the improvement of the quality of life for us all."

"Amen!" Matt and Jeff added in unison.

Kim brightened. "Our president is the leader of the free world. His or her sexual proclivities unless it is abusive, against the law or threatens our national security is of no interest to me. It's salacious gossip and childish."

Peter thoughtfully added, "Maybe."

"Maybe?" Kim was incredulous. "Are you aware that in 1993 we had the first World Trade Center bombing?"

Then Peter blew it! "That was nothing!"

"Nothing? I was at work in Manhattan that day -- people died.

If I remember correctly, a young pregnant woman and her unborn child lost their lives." Kim turned red.

"The perpetrators were caught quickly and prosecuted." I thought I'd better quell the situation. I was surprised by Kim's response.

"Several years later we had the attack on the World Trade Center in New York! Was that nothing?"

"I didn't mean…" Peter stammered

"Know your history, kid. These people are fanatics. They're patient and deadly. Did you know our guys had Bin Laden in their sights back then?"

"And," Peter continued.

"And distracted Clinton made a bad call and refused to act. Look where we are now!"

She had a valid point. Proudly, I announced, "And Kim helped with that too."

Kim was horrified. She leaned over and begged in a whisper, "Except for you and Brad, I've never told another soul."

"It's okay," I assure her, "the information was not unknown and quickly made public. You have nothing to worry about."

Matt and Jeff make some lame excuse and leave. They've reminisced enough and need to beer up their mugs.

"Tell me," Peter leaned in.

Kim looked to me for permission. I nod and encourage her to continue.

"Just after the World Trade Center attack, an acquaintance who knew I volunteered at the department asked if I could help someone who had vital information that might have been linked to the event. I agreed to meet with the person and introduce them to Jack, knowing he had contacts at the FBI." She pauses and measures her words carefully.

"After several unsuccessful attempts to meet, the person, terrified of perceived repercussions asked their contact to forget the entire incident and refused all help. Shortly thereafter my friend received a letter which included a bill from a local flight school with a notation on it and asked me to pass it on to Jack, which I did."

Peter was on the edge of his seat. "What did it say?" he prompts.

Kim is uncomfortable talking about it having promised to never reveal the information to anyone but me and Brad. I knew it was no longer important nor worth worrying over. I gave her permission to speak with another reassuring nod.

She discloses "It was the paid invoice from a local flight school which contained the list of names of men who took flying lessons. At the bottom of the page was a handwritten note by the flying instructor indicating the men refused to learn how to land the planes."

Unbeknownst to Kim that information was sent by the flight school owner to government officials and was well-known in all branches of law enforcement federal state and local. Peter wanted more information. There wasn't any.

We are running out of conversation and it is getting late.

The police department did a nice job of organizing the party and finding so many of the wonderful folks I worked with and for whom I have great respect. I've indulged and am now loosening my belt. I've been talking all night connecting and reconnecting to people who were such an important part of my life for many years. Kim too has reconnected with many people. We've had a great time. It's time to leave.

"Kim, Brad is waiting. I'll drive you home."

"Yes, thank you." Kim gratefully prepares to leave.

"Wait, Kim. Would you consider coming back to the department? I am in the Violent Crimes Division and we have some open cases. I see you two work well together," Peter says just above a whisper.

"Of course, Kim, you would have to repeat the vetting process with the FBI, but it could be interesting for you," he adds.

He prattles on as if he is in charge and doing us a big favor.

"Jack, we found new evidence on a case you consulted on after your retirement."

"Yeah. The John Banion/Harry Gellis murder case. I heard."

Peter seems upset that I know.

"What did you hear?" he demands.

Kim's eyes widen. She falls strangely silent. I can't read her non-response. It seems to be an odd mixture of surprise, wrapped in annoyance, tinged with fear and satisfaction. My senses are heightened.

"Just that there is new evidence in the case. So, what did you find?" I inquire.

Peter is happy now and assertive.

"New construction is being done in the area where Banion/ Gellis' bones were found."

Kim is visibly shaken. "Harry Gellis?" She blurts out.

It was her reaction at his name. For a moment, I wonder if she had anything to do with John Banion alias Harry Gellis meeting his maker. Oh, I know she didn't kill him, but I remember hearing he gave her some trouble and she was a fighter. Then again according to my buddies who worked at Pima Vista Retirement Village where they both lived, Harry Gellis was a nasty pain in the ass. He gave everybody a hard time.

I inform her. "Yes. His body or what was left of him was found near the private airport. Why? What do you remember?"

"He told me he was going to Mexico, and I just thought he left. I didn't know he was murdered."

Ninety-nine percent of my brain tells me she is innocent and knows nothing about his death. It's that irksome one percent that will keep me up tonight.

Peter is excited. "Believe it or not, an IBM phone issued in nineteen ninety-four was just found buried in the area where the body was found."

"Mmm. It could be an important clue," I muse.

"I didn't know they had mobile phones last century," Peter jabs.

Kim ignores his comment. With a trembling hand, she's already

226

done a search on her smart phone.

She reads, "It was the first smart phone, called the IBM Simon Personal Communicator. The price? Approximately $899, with a contract, $1,099.00. without."

Peter adds, "Our experts are trying to extract information from it."

"Wow!" Is all I can say. I'm thrilled and eager to be involved in the John Banion/Harry Gellis case. Kim not so much.

"Kim, this could be fun just like old times. What do you say?" I urge. Peter and I wait eagerly for her answer.

"No, thank you. I just don't have the time or the energy. I waited a long time before I started to write and there is where my focus lies for now. But I appreciate the offer."

"What are you writing?" I probe disappointedly.

"Screenplays. It's such an interesting way to tell a story," she says nonchalantly.

"Wow! I'm impressed. Why not a book?" I naively ask.

By her half smile, I know I just said something stupid.

"I may take up that challenge someday," she assures me.

I feel better.

Peter has been watching us. He directs his conversation to Kim and hands her his business card.

"Good-bye. It was nice meeting you and if you ever change your mind, I will keep a slot opened for you."

Non-committal Kim shakes Peter's hand and says, "That's very kind. Jack, are you ready?"

I take her arm and we depart.

"Your carriage awaits you, madam," I spout.

I don't know where that bunkum came from. My palms are sweating again. She just turns me on.

She seems amused and appreciative. We say our good-byes as we meet people on the way out.

I think I should change the subject. "Speaking of history, I never knew the full story about the gal with the terrorist boyfriend. Will you tell me now?"

She takes a deep breath and begins, "I guess it's time I'll tell you the full story. It was related to me during a routine check-up appointment with one of my doctors who was terribly upset and asked for my help. He knew I volunteered at the police department.

Respectful of the doctor/patient confidentiality rules and without revealing names he told me a young female patient had just been in to see him after she was brutally beaten by her boyfriend whom she had expected to marry. She was shocked and in disbelief about the attack. Having not told anyone, she confided to the doctor that she innocently began a relationship with the young middle eastern man she met in Las Vegas while on vacation. He followed her to Phoenix with promises that she read as ever-lasting love.

He eventually moved in with her. He was chauvinistic and had imposed definitive requirements for her to act, dress and behave as his woman. In the beginning she was flattered by his attentiveness and didn't mind his demands because he had come from a different culture and she assumed they would both adapt to each other's way of life. He was controlling but charismatic and philosophical about life.

Blinded by love and misplaced sympathies for his so called battle with prejudice she accepted his passionate outbursts, sometimes slovenly personal habits, and lack of social graces. She never knew how he made a living 'It is none of your business!' he would remind her every time she asked. But from time to time, he gave her small amounts of money to help with expenses.

At his insistence and intimidated by her own strict, religious father she kept her relationship a secret from her parents and friends until she had a ring on her finger which her boyfriend had promised and which she expected to happen quickly. Instead the young man became secretive, argumentative and abusive. He would disappear for days, used her credit cards without her permission or explanation, stole a significant amount of cash which she was saving to pay for the wedding, and in general, terrorized her. She felt trapped.

During one dangerous outburst, he apparently lost an important piece of paper. He tore the apartment apart accused her of going through his personal belongings, questioned her for hours and when he didn't receive the response he was looking for, he beat her so badly that she lost consciousness. He left her lying on the floor unconscious and bleeding. He made no attempt to help her. Instead, he removed all his belongings from her apartment and disappeared.

He left a hastily written threatening letter in which he swore she would never see him again and warned her not to even try to track him down or she and her family would be killed. By the time she regained consciousness several hours had passed. She immediately called a locksmith, changed the locks on her door, added locks to her windows and then went to see the doctor and confided in him.

The doctor treated her wounds, which according to him were extensive and encouraged her to go to the hospital and seek help from the police. She refused and begged him not to report the incident to the police partly out of fear, partly out of shame. That's when the doctor asked me to help. I offered to meet the girl. She dismissed that idea. I agreed to help without meeting her. She denied my help. The doctor and I realized the danger she was in and worried about her. I never knew her name, where she lived, or anything about her other than she feared for her life and soon disappeared.

Months later, the doctor asked me to come to his office. He received a letter from her with a piece of paper enclosed. The envelope had no return address and all postal markings were deliberately smudged. The doctor told me that shortly after the attack the girl fled the country and began work as a volunteer teaching English in some remote part of the world leaving friends, family, and colleagues wondering why.

The doctor handed me the key piece of paper shriveled and slightly shredded at the edges. It had actually been stuck in her vacuum cleaner and she had recently retrieved it. That 'lost' piece of paper resulted in the girl getting beaten. The doctor said that the girl in her letter indicated enough time had passed and asked that I get it to the right people."

"Did you ever find out what happened to the girl?" I asked.

"I followed up years later and to my knowledge the girl never returned to the United States, nor married and spent the rest of her life in self-imposed penitence working around the world helping others. I doubt that she ever shared her story with her family or friends. I can't imagine how this young woman has suffered."

"And the so-called boyfriend?"

"His name was the first on the list of young men taking flying lessons but refusing to learn how to land. I believe he is long gone."

63

The Prod

As I escort Kim to my car I ask, "How long have you been in Arizona?"

She seems surprised by my question. "You know perfectly well – it was 1994 just after you retired and took over the volunteer program."

Lamely I continue, "Oh, yes I remember. You were from New York, right?"

There it is-- the squint behind the glasses. Her personal detection device. She still absorbs information like a sponge, calculates and analyzes it all quickly and when she comes to some conclusion there is the squint.

"What's on your mind, Jack?" She knows I'm fishing.

Busted! I might as well go for it. "What do you remember about the John Banion/Harry Gellis case?"

Innocently she shares "The case? I didn't know there was a case. My time at the police department was spent in the pawn detail, the gang unit and for a time, I worked with the district attorney as he cleaned up the language of some outdated traffic laws. But you know all that. Why do you ask?"

"I thought you knew him," I say weakly.

This just isn't going right. Kim leans over and pats my hand. "Nobody really knew him. What I remember is that Harry Gellis was a bully who nobody took seriously. Many of the women he dated after his wife died found him (and I am being kind) difficult. And then he disappeared." She shrugs her shoulders, but I know she's frightened. "I honestly believed he went to Mexico."

"Why do you say that?"

"Because he told me that was his plan and then he was gone."

"My buddies at Pima Vista told me he gave you a hard time so why would he share his plans with you?"

"Maybe he wanted me to go with him."

"Oh. I didn't think of that. This may be our chance to close another case and get more bad guys off the streets."

Without a beat she reassures me, "Well, I am confident that with your skills and all the new technology you will find the answer."

I'm thinking maybe I am wrong about Kim but she's a bit off, nervous. She's hiding something. I'll just take her home and wait for some death-bed confession from the shooter. I switch on the radio. We drive the rest of the short way in silence. She's busy texting which amuses me. It's like watching my grandkids at Thanksgiving sitting at the same table and texting each other.

I walk her to her door. "Kim, it was wonderful seeing you again."

Brad opens the door iPhone in hand. "Hi you, two. Kim, I was just texting you back."

I smile as Kim takes out her iPhone and texts back. "Isn't modern technology great?"

She grins like a teenager. I watch as Kim and Brad embrace.

"Have fun?" Brad asks enthusiastically.

"Yes lots."

Brad places his arm around me and says, "Come in Jack. I prepared coffee, tea and…"

Kim adds, "Yes, do come in Jack. Let's tell Brad all about the speeches." All her energy goes towards Brad and she appears to be safe in his arms.

"Well, maybe for just awhile." I acquiesce. I'll have to leave soon, though and walk Lobo.

While I wish I was in Brad's place, I enjoy being around Kim and Brad as a couple – they bring so much love into the room. Brad, I admit is an attractive man with a smooth manner, a deep voice and a charming French accent. Kim once told me that on their very first date, Brad brought her flowers and continues to bring home a bouquet every Saturday night since. He's like Cary Grant. Women want to be with him; men want to be like him.

After about an hour I look at my watch. Kim picks up on it, winks at Brad and suggests, "Oh, Brad, you are such a good host. It's getting late. Jack needs to go and walk Lobo."

Brad gets up, shakes my hand and answers, "Yes, of course. I'm glad you two had such a good time. Now if you will excuse me, I need to get to bed. I have an early meeting tomorrow."

It was getting late and time for me to go home. I said my goodbyes and headed towards my car.

I heard Kim tell Brad, "No, Brad. I didn't tell him. Why ruin a lovely evening? Rest well, my love. I'll finish cleaning up and perhaps just stay up awhile."

I didn't understand what she meant but it was a pleasant ending to a wonderful evening. As I walked to my car, I kept thinking, how could Kim possibly be connected to the Gellis case? I'm going to drop it.

64

Kim and Brad are Gone

Unbeknownst to me that would be the last time I ever saw Kim. Six months later Brad called me to tell me she passed quietly in her sleep. He asked me to come by. He had something for me.

I was filled with an overwhelming sadness and dreaded the visit, but I honored his wish. Brad, as always, the gracious host, prepared tea and pastries for me. But he set the table for three as if Kim was to join us. Her presence was surely felt. It was eerie and comforting at the same time.

"How are you doing, Brad?" I inquired.

"Poorly. I miss the sound of her voice, her beautiful face, the warmth of her arms around me while we watched old movies. Our lives were so intertwined. We were inseparable and did everything together. She is simply the love of my life."

I was crying inside for him for me for Kim. For I knew she loved Brad, life in general and its simple pleasures. I needed to get out of there.

"Come to the office with me," Brad suggested.

I reluctantly followed Brad to their home office. It was brightly lit. Two desks sat side by side. One wall was filled with books. Antique and collectible research books on one side, books about writing on the other, and novels and biographies in the center. There were certificates of excellence on the walls for various writing contests and a crystal sculpture for first place in a screen-writing contest. Quietly

Kim amassed several awards which Brad pointed out with great pride.

"Kim wrote something you should see. It is related to an open case," he said sadly.

I was intrigued. Kim never took work outside the office and as far as I knew, shared everything work related with the people to whom she reported. She never gossiped with staff about individuals in the department or cases. She often said, "If you have nothing nice to say about someone, say nothing."

Brad handed me an envelope.

"She kept a diary when we arrived here in 1994. Read it! Gather whatever information you need from it and then destroy it," he instructed.

"I will," I promised.

We said our goodbyes. That would be the last time I saw Brad. Within three months, he was gone. They had no children and all their worldly goods went into a charitable trust. It would take a long while before I could read Kim's diary.

Eventually, with Lobo at my side, I read her diary. I had no idea Harry Gellis was such an animal. The unfortunate part of the story is that she probably felt guilty for Harry Gellis meeting his maker. She shouldn't have. There were guys all over Phoenix waiting for the right moment. They knew where he was and that he was planning to leave the country. Once he was separated from the Witness Protection Program, he didn't hide his whereabouts.

I feel badly that Kim suffered so. Had I known I would have taken care of Harry my own way. I just don't understand why she didn't confide in me. Oh, yes I do. I warned her about using any department resources for her own or anyone else's personal use.

She did the right thing, though. She filed a complaint with the Board, then with the police but without proof…That's often the problem with crimes against women and children, the lack of proof. Either the victim is too traumatized, embarrassed or scared to come forward or because the law requires witnesses. By the very nature of the crime, there aren't any witnesses. Hopefully, today with all the cameras, smart phones, watches and other recording devices, these types of crimes will cease or be easier to prove and prosecute. I'm furious.

65
The Sit-In

Soon after I finished reading Kim's diary, Peter the rising star in the police department called me to tell me, they uncovered evidence from the IBM phone issued in 1994 found in the desert near where John Banion/Harry Gellis' bones were found. It was registered to Carl Mitchello which I found out later is my Shadow Man.

He was transferred from NY to stand trial in Arizona for the murder of John Banion aka Harry Gellis. I was invited to witness the interrogation. He confessed everything and gave us a detailed description of Harry's last moments. He was tried and convicted. He sits in his cell and after finding God ministers to other prisoners who need his guidance.

They're all gone now, Kim, Brad, Harry Gellis, Willie the Weasel, and many of the people from the Pima Vista Retirement Community. Boys Night Out ended. Randi and Christine eventually married and moved to Tucson where Randi manages another development. I get Christmas cards every year and the last I heard, they were about to welcome their fifth child and were very happy.

Phil's house was condemned. His wife refused to go for therapy; Phil just walked away from the marriage and went back to long distance trucking.

Sean hooked up his trailer to his truck and he and Phil hauled it to Las Vegas where Sean relocated when the building boom happened.

Me, I'm thinking of moving to Pima Vista with Lobo who has been an integral member of my family since I adopted him. He accompanies me everywhere and has never left my side since he was a pup. We're both much older now—no more five o'clock a.m. six mile runs in the desert. Slow walks in the dog park are where we hang out with other dog enthusiasts who have become friends and occasional dates. My daughter and grandchildren are far more attentive than ever, and I get to see them often. They love Lobo and have inherited most of my sports equipment. It is a joy for me to see them grow and indulge in the same activities I did. I no longer have that hollow feeling in my soul.

I often think of Kim and Brad. They were a beautiful couple. Now when I look up at the night sky, I imagine them dancing in the moonlight.

THE END

AUTHOR'S NOTES

Simply, thank you to my readers.
Your support and positive reviews have encouraged
me and brought me great pleasure.

Soaring in Silence is a fictionalized version of stories
told to me by women who have been sexually and
physically abused. During their time of need in
decades past, help and support were not readily
available. If you or anyone you know has suffered the
trauma of abuse, please contact any of the following
sites and seek immediate help:

https://www.womenshealth.gov/relationships-
andsafety/get-help/state-resources

https://www.victimrights.org/

https://metoomvmt.org/

**For those of you who suffer from Vasculitis,
or know someone who does, please visit:**

www.vasculitisfoundation.org or call
1.816.436.8211 or 1.800.277.9474 Fax:
1.816.656.3838

https://rarediseases.org National Organization for
Rare Disorders

Printed in April 2023
by Rotomail Italia S.p.A., Vignate (MI) - Italy